Rococo

SUE HOLLISTER BARR

CONTENTS

ACKNOWLEDGMENTS

The artwork on the cover was done by
Josue Ledesma.

PART 1

SUE HOLLISTER BARR

*P*hys attend.

What a fucking waste of my time. Annoyed, I amused myself by combing my fingers through the cherubs dripping off the edges of the conference table. They were busy fornicating before I disturbed them, but the holography was sophisticated enough to respond to my touch. Since each was about the height of one of my fingers, they tried to couple with my fingers instead. I couldn't feel any of it, but when I idly tried to shake one off and hit the actual, phys table it did little to improve my mood.

"My dearest Nan, I trust no harm befell you?"

"Anybody with half a brain has Nusoft furniture," I snapped at my boss. "Especially now that Rococo's the rage, and there's really no way to know where the holo stops and the phys begins." I glared hard across the tabletop's riot of moving marquetry, which could have passed for phys wooden inlay if the animals hadn't been chasing each other.

Dressed like a Dickens character in his top hat, my boss had clamped his mouth shut hard. He was fidgeting with his magenta muttonchops.

Oh fuck, I'd done it again. My friggin' anger problem, one of the reasons an R&D genius like myself was currently working for a friggin' entertainment corp. This boss had been nothing but nice to me since I'd finally met him this afternoon. But even his clothes annoyed me. Not to mention the magenta eyes. I hated magenta eyes. Still, I really needed the yen. I had to stop seeing monsters where there weren't any. So I did my best to look sheepish while I said I was sorry and then plastered on a smile so inviting it may have erred on the side of come-hither.

My boss loosened and went back to blabbing about how the assignment I'd been slaving over forever meant so much to our great nation. I tried to listen, really I did, but I just couldn't take all that flowery language any more seriously than his clothes. Behind him paisleys, which weren't even Rococo but Victorian, crawled across the wallpaper. Why couldn't anyone ever get retro right?

A huge vaulted window showed the fan-like top of the Chrysler building. It was covered with semi-circular tiers of Gainsborough portraits, stately except the subjects were all chattering with each other. Two mag cars hovered not far below it, a testament to how low to the ground that historic building top was now. One of the mag cars looked like a peacock, foppish holo feathers flopping about everywhere, the other like a Pekingese, running through the air on stubby legs. I squinted at the window and frowned repeatedly.

My boss must have noticed and stopped talking again.

I tried to fix things again, nervously caressing the cherubs while I gave him another winning smile.

"Doubt not, my dearest Nan. Augmented 'glass' resists the sun's fiery rays at this latitude, but that window is indeed physical. As am I." He got up from his chair and headed toward me.

What was he going to do? Touch me and

maybe give me a disease? I couldn't wait to finish my assignment and move on to the next boss at the next corp. Who the hell held a meeting that required physical attendance, unless their corp's shit was top secret, or they wanted to kill you? All I wanted to do was go home to Alaska so I could continue to conduct both my business and personal life by projection like a normal person.

He took not one, but both of my hands and pulled me to my feet. I could just imagine all the germ sensors in my bloodstream going wild, though nothing beeped.

"Nan, my dearest dear," he intoned warmly. Then he fell silent, gazing into my eyes and seeming to wait for some kind of reaction.

With his fashionable cuffs of lace spilling over my hands, I felt naked, like a peasant in the simple brown suit that matched my tan. I couldn't be bothered with fashion. Years ago I'd just printed the first comfortable business suit I'd googled.

"You seem almost shy," he said at last. "It

becomes you. That unruly, delightfully rebellious mop of short brown hair is most fetching, really, and those sharp blue eyes... Natural, aren't they?"

I mumbled a yes.

"But of course. You look the natural type. Probably more at home in expedition wear, embarking on some extreme sport. Speaking of which, when was the last time you had sex with a person, not a projection? You, Nan, are a beautiful woman."

I snatched my hands back. "It's not safe!" But why was I being so unreasonable? When was the last time anyone offered me sex I didn't have to pay for? After all, he was risking incurable AIDS as much as I was.

He shrugged, sighed, and ran his fingers through the cherubs on his way back to his side of the table. "Forgive my impertinence. I'm so rarely in the presence of a physical person; I was quite overwhelmed. Your smiles, your affinity for the cherubs led me to believe...but alas, I was mistaken."

"Why *am* I phys here?"

"Ah, yes. *That*." I saw something hard

snap shut in his magenta eyes, and it was my turn to be overwhelmed by his phys presence. I actually shuddered while he tugged his earlobe and said "curtains" and I watched the Chrysler Building disappear behind thick drapery. No paisleys crawled, no animals scampered, and no cherubs fucked their way across its thick burgundy velvet. Was that huge drapery actually phys? "Your contract," he continued. "I'm quite pleased with your work on the star drive for our ship."

"But what you were so quick to prevent me from saying by projection is that it'll only work for a one-way trip!"

"That, my dearest dear, is precisely what I thought you were about to say." He looked at me intently, almost sadly, then shrugged and sighed again. "Now, here, you can tell me all about that."

I did. I told him all about the limitations of star drives, of TexMex's prophetic physicist from the last century with his ring around a sphere-shaped ship, of oscillating the bubble density, of sealing wax, of cabbages and kings.

He leaned across the table towards me,

propping his chin up in his palms. An inlaid antelope leaped gracefully over both of the elbows he rested on the tabletop; the lion chasing it sneaked beneath them. What my boss did not do, which I found surprising, was tug his earlobe and say "record." Still he did seem to be listening very intently to my every word. When I finished he asked, "So, there's absolutely no way anyone could return to tell the tale, and they'd be too far away to broadcast it?"

His uncharacteristically plain words sent a sharp shiver up my spine.

I'd thought it was a great contract: Help the planet by getting all the aliens back to their own planet and off our welfare system. Help myself by networking for future contracts with the filthy rich TexMexes funding it so they could go along for the extreme adventure. Of course that last had been working with the assumption, shared by the TexMexes, that the TexMexes would be coming back...

He must have seen my reaction. "My dearest dear, you can't possibly be thinking I asked you to physically attend this meeting of just the two of us so I could plunge a dagger—hologrammed up to look like a bouquet of posies—into your heart? Perhaps drag your corpse from the room looking like a rolled-up antique carpet, right out of some 21st century holo noir?"

I didn't respond. What desperate yearning for yen had compelled me to agree to a contract with an entertainment corp and a phys attend? Me, who never phys attended anything? Even my parents never phys met but only sent what was necessary to the lab that produced me.

"Nan," he continued, looking genuinely concerned. "Think about this logically. You're the undisputed top in your field, this is a momentous undertaking, and you of all people know you haven't yet given us enough to complete the ship's drive. Even if your unpersoned model did test perfectly." His face did look sincere and kindly. "Forgive me if trying to appeal to your sense of humor with the holo noir before was the wrong thing to do. I never dreamed—"

"The TexMex tourists?"

His temper erupted. "Those particular Tex-Mex tourists include key government officials in favor of further reclamation of the land they say we stole from them in the 19th century when their country was still called 'Mexico.' We're as well rid of them as we are those useless aliens. Two birds; one stone. Did you really want those rich, snobby Tex-Mex Nucastilians not only taking Texas back but going after Arizona and Numexico, too? In this global world has patriotism gone completely out of style? You're one of us— from the country that used to own all the land north of the Rio Grande—and we have to stick together."

So much for hitting the tourists up for future contracts. Seemed a shame to make them pay so dearly for their own banishment, but I suddenly had to suppress a laugh.

"What?" he asked, again looking concerned.

"Just wondering what the TexMexes will do on the aliens' planet. Go on welfare?"

He laughed way too heartily, way too

long, as if he were tremendously relieved about something. But it had only been a moment of gallows humor on my part, not all that funny. I was patriotic enough to hate what we used to call Mexico for "reclaiming" Texas, but stranding any human being on the aliens' planet was another matter. Living in family units was still the norm in TexMex, and they were bringing their children. Besides, I could feel irrational anger bubbling to the surface yet again and was ready to hate anyone. Again I glared across the table at my boss.

His laughter dissolved, a bit awkwardly. He must have realized no smile would replace the way I was looking at him this time.

A wooden hawk swooped down to capture a wooden rodent that failed to hide itself adequately behind the elbows he still rested on the tabletop.

I asked, "Am I free to leave?"

"But of course, my dearest dear!" He pulled back at last, taking his elbows off the table so the animals scampering across its surface no longer had to detour around them.

"All I ask is that you honor the confidentiality agreement in your contract, including one further stipulation: Say nothing about 'one way' to anyone, not even in my corporation."

"Agreed." Which was a lie.

His magenta eyes were cloaked in shadow as he stood back from the table. "Any other plans before going home?"

"None." Which was true.

"Then before you leave Manhattan you really must let me take you to an early dinner no simulator can match."

He didn't know my sim's culinary triumphs, or the yen that particular simulator had cost me. Typical antiquated city snobbery. I glared at him yet again.

He bowed, the soul of affability. "In a public place, to be sure, where death by holographically disguised dagger would be quite impossible, my dearest dear." Suddenly chagrined, he took to fidgeting with his hair again. "Or did I err yet again by trying to relax you by joking when your concerns should not be addressed in such a manner?"

Followed by a chance to see the view

from his apartment high up on the space elevator? Was he still interested in phys sex? But I figured if he'd meant me any harm, we wouldn't be preparing to leave this room with the phys curtains across the window.

No, I wouldn't go to his apartment and risk AIDS 7 or, looking at him, a common cold for that matter. But dinner in a public place should be safe. Besides, with my anger problem, could I even begin to trust that my feelings about this man were fair or accurate? It seemed like the entire workforce of the world was getting contracts faster than I could anymore, and I really did need the yen. After all the hostility I'd displayed, the least I could do in the interest of job security was to try to remember to smile at him—though not too beguilingly—across a dinner table. "Don't worry; it's fine. You're right; we have to stick together. And dinner would be nice. Just as long as we go now so I can get home to Alaska soon."

He looked like that wooden hawk had looked when it sank its talons into the rodent. But I shook it off, assuming it was just my imagination coupled with my anger problem.

He bowed deeply. "I am very pleased. We will leave momentarily. I have just a few things I must attend to first." He reached for his earlobe, then stopped. "Physically. You can wait with my new assistant." He winked and smiled. "In a public place."

His manner was comfortable and easy. Still, just to be sure, I spun about and stood right in front of the door. It didn't open. Just as it occurred to me that, like the drapery, nothing on it was moving, he reached around me and actually turned and pulled the doorknob to open it. He then escorted me out with another bow.

The hall no longer featured the chariot races through the clouds that it had when I came in. Instead, rosy-cheeked 18th century peasants frolicked in the woods amidst waterfalls. It even faux physed—though faintly, like some sex site so cheap it couldn't actually take your virginity away—the water spray I could just barely feel on my arms.

My boss phys opened another door and ushered me into a windowless room where nothing moved. I hesitated by the door, about to bolt back into the hall, till the woman standing in a dress, so wide and long that she couldn't possibly sit in it, turned around.

"My assistant. I'll be right back." He closed the door behind us.

When we were alone I grinned from ear to ear. "Trix, you got the contract! I'm so glad I suggested you contact this corp about their opening, my friend. I was starting to worry that you might never—"

"Were you addressing me?" There was just the faintest hint of a Southern drawl. Innocent eyes full of springtime widened.

"Who else would I—" A cold chill passed through me. Germs be damned. I grabbed the woman before me and quickly ran my fingers over her facial features before she had time to react.

"I beg your pardon!" She shoved me back.

I hit the sharp corner of a cabinet that was, regrettably, all too phys. But what I'd felt on her face matched what I saw. I'd even felt the hoops of that impossibly wide dress of hers against my legs. Looking around, I didn't think there was a shred of holo in the whole room.

"Forgive me. I just had to be sure it was really you, Trix." Grinning again, I was still puzzled. "But who had to slap my favorite slut silly to get you to wear anything that covers your butt, let alone hits the floor?"

"Whatever you could be talking about I really cannot imagine." Trix pushed some ringlets off her face.

"Okay," I said, "I get it. Another black market personality. And I was just getting used to Trix, the consummate slut. Who are you supposed to be this time? Scarlett O'Hara? Their languatician should be shot. No duel, no twenty paces, right in the back."

"Have I had the pleasure of making your acquaintance?" she queried sweetly.

"We've been best friends for 20 years."

Trix looked blank.

"Does the name 'Nan'—oh never mind mine—does the name 'Trix' mean anything to you?"

Trix still looked blank. "I do truly believe they gave me a partial memory wipe while I was there."

No shit.

"The people at the Hush-Secret Nuperson Discount Outlet were most considerate," she declared with more conviction than she'd previously been able to give anything. "They helped me understand how it would be ever so much easier to adjust to my new personality that way."

This infuriated me no end, and I was pretty sure it wasn't my anger problem. "Of all the shoddy— I don't believe you did this to yourself again. How many times have I quoted link and site when detailing the dangers of personality work and the very good reasons why it's illegal?"

"Pooh!" Trix countered. "I'll recall names in a minute, just see if I don't. Why, I just now came out from under the machine at the Hush-Secret Nuperson Discount Outlet up yonder." Trix feigned pulling her earlobe as if I were a small child who didn't know how to make a call. "You just say 'Hush-Secret

Nuperson Discount Outlet' and they'd be just tickled pink to give you an additional twenty percent off if you get a full personality reconstruction before Mars Day."

I had to smirk. "Remarkably selective, those memory wipes..."

"Don't be cross at poor lil'...Trix! That's my name! See? A person's always a little foggy after memory work. You know they take away a little too much memory on purpose because some of it comes back, but I'm mighty glad I did it. You all can be, too! The Hush-Secret Nuperson Discount Outlet's offices are right over yonder at—"

"No, thank you. You can keep your discount personality houses to yourself. At least when you bought your slut personality from Spice of Life they had the decency to do their research. For myself, I'm having enough trouble with reputable therapies, not the kind of sleaze-ball shit you have to phys attend. I got a Feelings Flush from Sachs last week and I still can't get rid of all this fucking anger." I shook with rage, breath whistling through clinched teeth. As the shaking subsided I plumbed my depths for a legitimate source of outrage.

Birdlike, Trix tilted her head to watch.

Though the images of an old pipe and a red ball flitted through my mind I came up empty-handed, as always.

Trix pouted, presumably on my behalf.

"Do you think it was that Assertiveness implant?" My anger was beginning to bubble to the surface again, faithful as a geyser. "I felt so good, so strong and powerful at first. But maybe it was of poor quality and turned on me later. Or maybe it didn't mix well with that fucking Positive Thinking I got last spring."

"Don't think about that now," said Trix. "You can always think about it tomorrow."

There was a rustling behind me. I turned to see the boss, who had swept off his top hat in a deep bow, his magenta curls tumbling toward the floor. The door to the hall was wide open, but now the peasants and waterfalls were gone. The diagonal tiles of a huge floor stretched into the distance, bathed in golden light. Here the faux phys consisted of hearing strains of the sweet music the elegant 18th century musicians played in their spacious chamber.

Still I snapped, "How long have you been standing there?"

"My dearest dear, you are among friends." He really did look sad, looking at me.

Well that was at least half true. But I hadn't even gotten the chance to tell Trix about my phys attend with the boss.

The boss stood to the side of the doorway and indicated I should exit to the hall with an elaborate flourish of his hand. "Perhaps you'll feel better after a good dinner, Nan. Trix?"

Trix looked confused, but only momentarily. "Yes?"

"Early dinner at the new Four Seasons, atop what used to be the Seagram Building. They even physically recreated the Pool Room, the original of which is now, ironically, under water. Care to join us? If, of course, you've completed that assignment I gave you just before you left for lunch?"

"What assignment?" Now Trix really looked confused.

"Ah," said the boss, starting to close the door with Trix still inside the room, but the two of us in the hall. "In the instructions I left you. Maybe next time."

Walking down the hall he stuck a bent elbow out toward me. It took me a moment to remember enough vintage vid to realize I was supposed to hook my hand around it, at which point I ignored it anyway for fear of germs. He looked up and down the empty hall, then stopped.

"My dearest dear, I mean you no harm. Truly I don't, Nan. I didn't mean to eavesdrop, but I did overhear what you told my assistant. And I did note your almost constant anger during our meeting. Much as I would enjoy an early dinner with you I wonder if it's really the best use of your remaining time before going back home to Alaska."

I thought I'd known what to make of him: enemy. But this was why I was far better off not phys attending anything, not having to conduct much, if any, business in real time. That way I could do it all in the morning before my eruptions of anger wore me down, robbing me of any objective perspective.

I was so damn sick of this shit. I could feel my shoulders sagging.

"I...do have a problem," I confessed, much to my surprise. I didn't even flinch when he again touched me, this time on my shoulders, as if trying to hold them up for me. It was a gesture I recognized from long ago, when I was a little girl whose shoulders often dropped in the face of a solar system I didn't feel I could understand.

My germ sensors remained quiet.

"I can help. If you would like, that is. I...had a similar problem." His hands rubbed my shoulders gently. It wasn't sexual. It was a gesture I remembered so well I had to blink back tears. My wonderful Grandpa of Oz.

"I've tried every reputable therapy there is," I blurted out. "Repeatedly."

"Believe me, I understand. I tried all that, too."

"If every reputable therapy in the solar system does nothing, what can I possibly do?"

Now he held my shoulders firmly, as if

trying to relieve me of the burden of standing on my own two feet. "Try something disreputable. Something deep. Something genetic."

I looked deep into those magenta eyes. At first I thought I saw that hawk in them but I'd probably imagined it both times, anger-induced paranoia. Now his look seemed so warm, so truly solicitous. He was speaking more simply, as if trying to accommodate my preferences. There was even a glint of humor, a little boy dying to share an inside joke, a secret none but the two of us could ever know.

He sported a phony stern look. "But you will have to," he paused to wink at me, "physically attend."

"But genetics are so unstable in personality work. They've made a mess of," I caught myself, not wanting to jeopardize Trix' new contract, "a friend of mine."

"But that's for personality work. You're not the kind who wants to wake up tomorrow talking and thinking like Marie Antoinette, are you?" he chided.

"But genetics, even used for behavioral work, are illegal."

"True," he said solemnly. "But that, my dearest dear, is far more political than safety-related. They just wave the flag of safety because they know that will silence the naysayers. They group them all together, personality alteration and behavioral and other therapies, so the known dangers in personality work can justify making them all illegal."

"Why?"

He leaned in so close I could feel the warmth of his body. With his hands supporting my shoulders I was flooded with memories of my Grandpa of Oz.

"Why?" he repeated. "Because a corp like your Sachs, who make a zillion yen a minute selling and reselling Feeling Flushes, make substantial donations to research facilities that group personality and behavioral work together."

"No," I snapped, anger gushing back up again, no matter how inappropriately. "A reputable corp like Sachs?"

He moved back a bit, giving me space. But his expression remained kindly, despite my glaring at him, just like in the conference room. As consistent as Grandpa O's grin.

"Your choice of course," he said quietly. "I'm just trying to help because I used to have an anger problem so very bad that it made yours look like nothing."

"Yes, but Sachs?"

"Think about it logically: You felt great after your first Feelings Flush, right?"

I nodded.

"That's the initial hook, just like centuries ago when they used to put wax in shampoo to make your hair shine. Works at first, but the accumulation has just the opposite effect later."

"So why would anyone continue to use such a shampoo?"

"Because it's human nature to stick with the original assessment despite all future evidence to the contrary. You stayed with Sachs, didn't you?"

He had me there.

Then the anger drained out of me

completely, and I was again left with drooping shoulders he reached out to support. "At least talk to some geneticists about it while you're here? Since it's illegal they can't say much over the phone..."

"Oh...all right."

He was that little boy again, thrilled like some kid brother in an old vid when the big kids let him join them. Twirling me around, he started us down the hall while its wallpaper played a Scarlatti concerto in D that soared, stirred me, and filled me with new confidence. Ah, the exuberance of the Rococo! With an arm around me, my boss proclaimed, "The time hath come to part with the old, and ring in the new."

But I saw a sign dead ahead, on the door at the end of the hall, "Warning: Public Walkway." I pulled back.

"What's wrong?" my boss asked, but he was still pushing me forward excitedly.

"An uncontrolled sidewalk?"

Jovial, conspiratorial, he leaned in to whisper, "Nobody calls them that anymore, since they're not at the side of anything anymore."

"But—"

"They're more like balconies and catwalks all over the place."

"But it's a public space with no privacy controls."

He was still hurrying me toward the door. "Can't exactly plug an illegal destination into a mag car, can we?"

"But a public walkway..."

"You can't chicken out now."

"You expect me to expose myself to...?"

But he was already pushing me through the door.

I stepped outside gingerly.

The ads hit before I'd fully exited the building. Gorgeous holo men, carefully tailored to fit every preference I'd ever revealed on a sex site, crowded around me, trying to pick me up. Next came a phys karate chop to my shoulder, fortunately not at all skillful. A phys adolescent was crossing my path, obviously amusing himself with a holo martial arts match only he could see as he walked along. Looking around I saw what I

believed to be more phys people crowded into
the same space than I ever wanted to see
again. Almost all, like the boy, were
gesticulating wildly in the air as they
walked...playing invisible musical instruments
with rhapsodic smiles, rowing invisible boats,
playing invisible sports while screaming at
invisible teammates. It reminded me of an
ancient vid I'd seen once that showed the
inmates in something called an asylum.

"47.88/21.45/98.30," said my boss as we
walked. I couldn't imagine how he could find
an address in the midst of whatever ads were
accosting him. I couldn't even see him past
my ads, half concealing him while the other
half made faux phys attempts at pulling me
away from him. But I was comforted when I
noticed my boss' hand holding my elbow tight
as he guided me.

"How many meters?" I asked.

He squeezed my elbow. "Not many, and
they're all horizontal."

"You using GPS?" I asked.

"No. Even talking with a geneticist about
treatment is illegal. Don't want to leave more

of a trail than we have to."

I doubted the hordes getting black market personality work bothered with such nuances, but said nothing. Address locations were required by law, and I thought they were supposed to be at eye level, but couldn't see any. My boss had to steady me when I tried to look around a holo "Star Cruiser" someone was trying to sell me. Jupiter's failed star, I knew damn well it couldn't get off the ground, let alone escape the planet.

"Look down," said my boss.

Ah. The trip-hazard law. No ad could intrude within a meter of your feet. So there, ringed by holo hiking boots for sale, I could just barely see the meter markings.

"47.85/21.44..." my boss read. He took us a meter sideways. "47.85/21.45."

I was following along with him now, though I had to admit I was momentarily distracted by a perfect pair of boots for the tundra surrounding my arctic home.

"47.86, 47.87, 47.88."

He pushed me through what I could only hope was a doorway since I couldn't see anything past an ad for a hotel high in the space elevator. Just before the ads vanished one of the gorgeous holo men threw a dozen roses at my feet, which disappeared before hitting a sterile white floor.

Nothing was moving. I reached out and touched what had to be a phys white wall. What a relief. I actually smiled at my boss.

He winked. "This way." He led me to a solitary white chair. "Here, have a seat."

I did.

"I'll be right back," he said.

Suddenly something seemed terribly wrong. For the first time since I was a child being raised, phys, by my Grandpa O, I reached out for another person, my boss. Or at least I tried. My hand got no farther than a few inches from the chair's arm rest before a white restraint became visible around my wrist. Frowning, I put my hand back on the arm rest. The restraint disappeared.

My boss had paused in the doorway to watch. "Surgical restraints. Routine. Don't worry."

"But I haven't agreed to anything. I

haven't even had anything described to me that I could agree to."

A woman appeared behind him, dressed in white. I could see from her natural face and plain hair that she was a scientific type like me, and with as little use for fashion. She checked my boss out from head to toe and rolled her eyes behind his back. When she started to speak I was expecting something like, "What the fuck do you have her in a surgical chair for?" Instead what she really said was a tired, bored, please-let-me-get-back-to-my-research, "So when you were here a few minutes ago you said you wanted—"

My boss had clamped a hand over her mouth, gesturing toward me.

She slapped his hand away. "To continue, hopefully without your having just contaminated me with an incurable disease..." I could tell she was pausing to listen for any beeping from the germ sensors swimming around in her bloodstream. "You said you wanted permanent removal of all her memory from the time you first spoke to her to the moment she goes under. That means we could tell her now that we're going to cut her up in pieces and throw her over a public walkway railing and it wouldn't matter, right?"

"You fucking pieces of shit!" I screamed. I banged my wrists and ankles against restraints that only became visible when I fought.

My boss looked at me. "Sorry, but I didn't believe you when you said you'd honor your confidentiality agreement, and you shouldn't have believed me when I said I was your friend." Amidst my screams, I saw what I thought was a hint of remorse before his gaze dropped to my body, and I figured it was only disappointed lust. Then I saw what I had not been mistaken about earlier when something very hard snapped shut in his magenta eyes. He took the woman-in-white's elbow and started to lead her away from me, out into the hall, despite her shaking him off. Somehow I didn't think his hand falling to her butt was a mistake. "Perhaps I'm just squeamish," he said to her, "but I'd rather some privacy when we sort out the details of the rest of what we're going to do to her,

Syb." He shut the door behind them.

My earlobe. If I could call Trix, who thought we were at the Four Seasons, or anyone for that matter. I couldn't free a hand to pull my earlobe, or even use a foot, but could I trigger the phone by dragging the side of my head against something? Unlikely, but not being able to think of anything else, I tried. A head restraint materialized as I banged my head around but, intelligently, they'd designed it so it wasn't possible to come even close to having anything touch an earlobe.

The room. Anything live in it that would respond to voice command? Again, unlikely, but I tried shouting them all, including all the emergency ones that were supposed to work in the deadest of rooms. Nothing.

My own internal sensors? How? Voice command to a sim and somehow get it to print and deliver something illegal, like live bubonic plague? Guzzle it down and wait for it to trigger an emergency broadcast from the germ sensors in my bloodstream?

The woman in white came back into the

34

room.

Futilely, stupidly, I banged everything I could against the restraints.

"He wasn't kidding; you are a fighter. But we're about to fix that." White walls pivoted to reveal lab equipment and operating room paraphernalia that had been hidden on the other sides. As far as I could tell, everything was phys, right down to a vintage clock. The time was 1732.

"Shame." The woman was looking at me, shaking her head. "You are so screwed." She started punching buttons. The chair I was held captive on started to recline, converting itself into an operating table. "And your boss is such a dick."

"Please, help me, somehow! I'll give you anything you want. I've got enough yen stashed away—"

"Don't even bother."

"You don't like him any better than I do. He has no real appreciation for science; he's not our type."

"He funds my research on telepathy."

"Please, we're the same kind of people,

you and me. I thought my research was going to get humanity to the stars. Instead—"

"Spare me." She turned her back on me, working on equipment I couldn't see. "Besides, humanity won't need anything we can't find in our own solar system for centuries."

The same rationale every reputable corp I'd proposed building a star drive for had used to turn me down.

"It's simple: fill the order exactly as requested by the sleazoid entertainment corp you were stupid enough to take a contract with, or lose the funding for my telepathy research." She paused to frown over, then remove, a torn fingernail.

"But he's a dick," I protested. "You said it yourself. So it shouldn't be hard for you to believe that I've done nothing to deserve this. And you yourself say I'm totally screwed. Come on, we're both scientists. Surely there's something, something you can do to help me."

She looked like she was about to yawn, having undoubtedly heard such speeches before, but suddenly stopped to look at me, as if for the first time. Did I imagine a smile toying with the corners of her mouth?

"Of course no one said I couldn't add a little something extra." As if inspired she again turned her back on me to work furiously on the equipment I couldn't see. "About time I get something out of all this silliness."

The restraints tightened so I couldn't move at all, and something punctured my arm. My tongue flopped about in my mouth and I couldn't talk anymore. I could still keep my eyes open, though just barely, and see the clock. The time was 1746. It was then I noticed this corp's name above its clock: Hush-Secret Nuperson Discount Outlet. I bit my own tongue yelling, "Trix!"

In my dream I could see Grandpa O again, each hair of his straight brows and every nuance of his wonderfully complex eye color, grey with a secret depth of khaki green, sparkling in the sunlight. As always, the soggy stub of an illegal cigar was jammed into the corner of his Teddy Roosevelt grin. He fiddled furiously with his jury-rigged electronics and winked at me, saying for the umpteenth time, "Pay no attention to that little man behind the curtain." Something beneath his backyard workbench sputtered, he kicked it, and the world around us disappeared. In its place was a holographic projection of the world I'd made up in my latest story. And I'd thought he'd been snoozing when I read it to him.

My eyes fluttered open. I was in my bed at home. Must have dozed off. Grandpa O in his backyard had only been a dream.

My clock read 2352. That was funny... I must have dozed off and slept all day. And I didn't even remember lying down. The last thing I remembered was that stupid underling from work, Reg, calling me about my stupid new contract for an entertainment corp, of all things, wanting a star drive. He'd complimented me on my work to date and told me the boss I had yet to talk to for the first time would be calling me in a few minutes, but the boss never called. Or I'd napped right through it. I rolled over in my bed and double pulled my earlobe, noting that my wrist seemed sore. "Messages?"

Strange. My tongue felt sore, too, as if I'd bitten it in my sleep, but the sound of my own voice had been even stranger. There had been just the faintest hint of a British accent. But anyway my house was quiet; there weren't any messages. I yawned, told my house to "dim for sleep," also in a faint though somewhat incorrect British accent, and dozed back off to sleep.

Just before waking I had another dream about Grandpa O. But he wasn't as I'd known him, the antiquated gentleman who'd raised me like only grandparents and bots did then because my generation's parents weren't interested. It was my grandfather as I'd never known him, as I'd never really believed he'd ever been, but I'd kept the old flat pic anyway because of the fire blazing in his cool grey eyes. In my dream, as in the pic, he was magnificently young, full of—as he would have put it in his archaic way—piss and vinegar. His hair was sandy brown, snapping about smartly in the breeze, like Peter O'Toole's in the vid *Lawrence of Arabia* that he was always showing me. Then he blinded me with his smile and sent a thrill all through me. Part of me knew it was a dream, yet he seemed more real than not only the best holo but even anyone else phys. He leaned in close, sending a shiver of excitement up my spine as I once again caught the scent of his whiskey-laced breath and felt the warmth of him close to me. "Remember everything," he hissed. "And to thine own self be true."

What the fuck was that supposed to mean? My eyes fluttered open and I heard my little glass house hum awake with me. It let in some sunlight, dappling the sim-wood floorboards, which I'd printed and installed myself, with moving patterns of light and dark. The shade pattern I'd picked simmed partial shade from the gently moving leaves of giant trees that didn't exist. Otherwise I included no holo in my décor. Padding through the swirling leaf patterns in my bare feet, I noted that even my ankles were sore. Damn, I must have slept funny. And I never made it out of my brown business suit, which I would have had no reason for wearing since

I hadn't left home. I didn't even remember putting it on—or anything else, for that matter—after that stupid underling from work, Reg, called. Though nothing beeped I double-checked my germ sensors' log, again with an inaccurate British accent. There was no sickness to explain how long I'd slept.

I then stepped up to the wall and waited for it to make a hole for me. I hadn't picked the best spot; my garden's flowers and shrubbery were pretty thick and hard to walk through as I stepped out into the Arctic morning. But the openness of the Alaskan wilderness stretched out beyond my garden's wall. I was glad to see that, despite the latest figures on the growing population in the region, I still couldn't detect any sign of other people. My closest neighbor, an owl, dive-bombed me. Years ago he'd terrified me with his five-foot wing span. Now I smiled up at the curves of his wide, art noveau face, sure he was winking at me with his yellow eyes. *Please, Nan, pretend to be frightened.*

These owls were still referred to as "snowies," though they had adjusted to global warming by becoming much less white. They'd also adjusted to increased competition from other predators with an insane mania for protecting their food sources. But he was only trying to impress his mate since he knew I had never eaten even one of his precious Alaskan Nurats. To the rats' relief, as they scampered back into their burrows, the snowy soared out over the glittering water far below that was now ice-free year-round. Some sea farming was just barely visible on the horizon.

I smiled softly in the sunshine. Grandpa O would have loved it here. Then I frowned. If he'd chosen to remain on this planet.

I was interrupted by a buzz in my ear. Reluctantly I pulled my earlobe, not waiting to hear who was calling. But the projection that hid a particularly lovely rose bush was immediately forgiven since it was my dear, currently consummate-slut, friend Trix. Except I didn't get the dress.

"Do I know you?" she asked. Huh? I didn't get the only marginally accurate French accent, either.

"I'm your best friend," I answered.

Damn. My own words still had a faint British accent.

"Best friend?" Trix stretched her arms toward me, getting as close as any projected holo phone call could. "Help me!"

"Trix?" Still the British accent.

"Who's Trix?" Still the French accent.

Long dress. White powder covering Trix' face and white hair piled high atop her head. "Marie Antoinette," I said. I started to add, "Okay, I get it, another black market personality; super slut is gone," but was stopped by an odd feeling. It reminded me of when I first discovered I could move a top segment of one of my toes independently, some vestigial skill from my ape ancestors. It had felt all creaky and weird, like some startlingly new path through my nervous system was being used for the first time. What came out of my mouth was, "Look here, I have bought this bonnet. I do not think it is very pretty, but I thought I might as well buy it as not. I shall pull it to pieces as soon as I get home, and see if I can make it up any better." Huh? Was that Lydia Bennet in *Pride and Prejudice*?

But Trix was crying. If I was going to help my friend, I had to get something other than still-half-asleep nonsense out of my mouth. "There, there," I managed.

"I don't even know who you are!" Trix exclaimed. At least she wasn't using Marie Antoinette's speech patterns. Wide-eyed and twitchy, she was more the sweet nerd-child— that last because she was robot-raised—than I'd seen since her insecurities about attracting men prompted her to try multiple black market personalities. "I've just been calling everyone in my contact list. I got my boyfriend..." Boyfriend? I didn't know Trix had a boyfriend. "...Mart. He's coming over, phys. But I can't wait. I'm going insane. And now that I'm talking to you something in my head hurts horribly." Sobs racked her.

I just had to say something useful but— that odd toe-moving feeling again—suddenly I was feeling slighted because Trix hadn't congratulated me about buying a...a bonnet?

Trix went on. "Mart made me promise not to call any more names, and made me tell him the names of everyone I'd already called, in case I'd done myself some damage. But I couldn't wait. And he was so adamant." Her usual nervousness was about to reach escape velocity. "You won't tell him I called you, will you? Will you? I'm afraid. Maybe," she bit her lip, spraying her white face powder as far as the edges of her projection range, "he won't want to be my boyfriend any longer."

I couldn't understand why anyone who'd experienced the faux phys enhancements of even a third-rate porn site would want a real, phys boyfriend. Maybe it was some odd transference since Trix had never had anyone phys in her life, except me. For her alone I risked disease since I could tell how much my phys presence meant. I tried over and over again to give her everything my Grandpa O had given me.

But I always went to her place; she'd never set foot in mine.

"Why aren't you saying anything? You are going to tell Mart. You are. I can tell by your silence!"

I couldn't say anything. Every time I tried

to say more than a few words I got that odd toe-moving feeling and knew whatever came out would be nonsense. Or was it nonsense? That occurred to me as the toe-move feeling returned. Maybe I had it all wrong, thinking Trix was the one who deserved the attention, when it was really me and my bonnet. The toe-move feeling receded. But what bonnet? Maybe just a few words at a time. "Trix..."

"Is that my name?"

"Yes."

"What's yours? I forget where I was in my contact list."

"Nan."

"Will you tell that I called you, Nan?"

"Mart? No."

"Are you sure, Nan?"

"I promise."

Trix startled as her gaze jerked to the side and behind me. "What is that? Look out!"

Was my neighbor back for more aerial acrobatics, at least pretending to be the maniacal protector of his family's food sources he was supposed to be? Following Trix' gaze I turned to check behind me but no

snowy owl was visible. The only thing
moving was—

I could hear Trix starting to
hyperventilate. I'd spent hours at her place
cradling her in my arms once that started, her
suffering unimaginable. This I had to stop,
now. Enough determination welled up in me
and I could speak freely. "Trix, you don't
mean the alien my garden maintenance corp
sent over, do you?"

"Your garden maintenance corp sent over
a man-eating alien just because bots can't
garden worth a damn?"

"Trix, how deep into memory did they dip
this time? You don't remember when we
discovered that what we thought were human
remains in their ship were really their alien
masters, much more like us than these docile
workers?"

"Run, Nan!"

"They're harmless! Their masters resorted
to cannibalizing themselves after the crash.
Most of the workers are dying slow,
expensive-for-our-welfare-system deaths. The
few who have yet to succumb to the rigors of

this planet couldn't even explain how to fix their own ship."

"Oh yeah, bot brain? Then how come the masters didn't eat their docile workers first? How come not a single 'master' was left alive, but all the workers survived?"

"Trix, please, breathe slowly. It was all explained later but for now: What's the alien behind me doing? Gardening?"

"No. It's looking at you. With blood on its mouth."

"Baring the teeth they showed us they don't have? Creeping toward me through the tundra, perhaps? Or is it just contemplating the odd lifeforms of Planet Earth?"

Judging from Trix' lower respiration rate, I thought I'd succeeded until she was distracted by something I couldn't see or hear and started to hyperventilate all over again. "Nan, my boyfriend's here! You promised not to tell Mart I called you, right?"

"That's absolutely right. I prom—"

Trix was gone, though not before I saw her fingers whip through the extra steps to perm erase our call.

I was glad she remembered that much. But I was still as worried as a drunk on a space elevator balcony. To have forgotten the whole alien deal? Even when Trix got Lolita, her first personality, she hadn't forgotten that far back. And my research, prompted by worry about Trix, indicated that was when the memory loss should have been the greatest. I needed to investigate further. Shame sensors and bots had put every last healthcare corp out of business. But maybe some corp had finally figured out how many yen could be made repairing the wreckage from black market personality work.

So much for my morning stroll through the tundra.

Or my weird dreams and garbled morning thinking and speaking.

I picked a better path through my garden than I'd landed on coming out of my house and stood by the exterior walls I left clear for lack of neighbors. No, I hadn't stupidly left any obstruction close to the interior wall this time. It made a hole for me. Starved, I stepped in and headed for my sim before I started researching.

I had just printed Coca Cola's beef stew—enough to make up for not eating most of the previous day and maybe a few days before that—when an odd feeling pricked the back of my neck.

"Ee-soose me, pease?"

I spun around. It was such an odd sound. Though the garden maintenance corp had sent over several aliens, I'd never heard one speak. They said it was because Universal English was physically painful for them.

Still dirty from working in the garden, it had moved close enough to the house to open a portal. At first I thought it was a mistake, but it stepped into the hole its presence had made in my house. I wasn't a vet, but I noticed it was dramatically thinner than other aliens I'd seen. All huge eyes slanting upwards. I certainly wasn't knowledgeable enough to comment on blue skin, but it looked dull, unhealthy, and more grey than blue.

"Yes?" I said.

It seemed to waver.

Not knowing how to field an unexpected phys visit from anyone or anything, I finally remembered a line out of an old vid. "Come in."

I regretted it the minute I said it; I so resented the intrusion of anything alive in my living space. It was creepily unnatural. A home was supposed to be a sanctuary where nothing existed but yourself and extensions thereof. This was something out of an old vid where people lived in groups that even included live, unpredictable animals.

It came toward me. Nothing, except for me, had ever walked across my hand-installed floor before. Was it unsteady on its...I guess you'd call those two things...feet? Or did it just have the most peculiar gait I'd ever seen, like a very slow skip? As it got closer the hairs went up on the back of my neck. I realized fully, on more than an intellectual level, that this was phys. I could hear its frenzied breathing and remembered learning somewhere that this was necessary because the gases it needed were in very short supply in our atmosphere. But what turned my stomach was the smell of what I slowly realized were the alien gases it exhaled. When it got within inches of me its eyes took on an odd intensity, and its beak-like mouth, which seemed to have blood smeared on it, spasmed. I wondered, nuttily, if it was going to kiss me. Instead it exhaled sharply, causing me to gag, feel faint, and understand why they didn't work with humans in confined spaces.

"Me food card." It shook from the effort of articulating "card." "Corp..." It paused again, grasping its throat. That last word seemed to have drawn its equivalent of blood. "...can not make work." It collapsed, sprawled like a broken thing across my floor.

The first thing I noticed was silence, then the dissipation of the vile smell, since it wasn't breathing. I ear-pulled a call to the garden maintenance corp, only half paying attention as I reported the situation. They went on forever about how something like that had never happened before, how well they treated the aliens, and how they were all members of the Green Party. Finally they said they'd be phys there in minutes to remove the corpse.

But I'd been watching the alien carefully throughout the call. True, it wasn't breathing, but there was something about it. I squatted beside it and finally spotted it, a slight quivering just below an armpit. Some sort of random rigor mortis? I checked the other armpit: same thing. And both were getting uniformly stronger and more pronounced.

It scrambled to its feet, resuming its fury of breathing and bathing me, still on the floor, with its odious exhalations. Steadying itself on my sim, it dipped three long, six-jointed fingers into my food...by accident, judging from its reaction.

I was gagging. I worried that I might pass out before I could get to my feet, but I got out of my mouth, "Try it; it's not bad."

It wasn't hot—I hated hot food—but clearly it found Coca Cola's beef stew as toxic as its exhalations were to me. Its struggles to quickly divest itself of every last speck of the stuff almost landed it on the floor again. It even exclaimed something that sounded like "dead."

I managed to get to my feet, though it put

me much closer to the source of toxic fumes than I wanted to be. The alien seemed trancelike, barely conscious of what it was doing. Still, when its gaze fixed on me I saw that odd intensity again. "Alive," it managed to say clearly, reaching for me. Then it dropped once more to the floor.

PART 2

SUE HOLLISTER BARR

uzz.

I jumped in my dream, already one of those nerve-wracking ones where everything goes wrong. I was forgetting something really important about my star drive but couldn't figure out what.

Trix.

The first of escalating announcements, it wasn't enough to wake me, only enough to reprogram my dream. Trix scampered out of my star drive, younger than I'd ever known her. A cute little kid with that mechanical walk—and tendency to fall down a lot—of the robot-raised.

Trix.

Louder. It occurred to me this might be coming from the outside world. Eyes still closed, I double-pulled my ear. "Time first."

0304.

But by then I was awake enough to remember that for Trix I didn't care what time it was and straight-pulled my ear. "Trix, why haven't you called me back?" I sat up in bed, yawned, and realized I could still smell that alien's exhalations even though the garden maintenance corp had removed its corpse a week ago.

"Nan."

Remembering my name was a good sign.

"Do not be...upset. Mart has been with me for...many days." Her grin threatened to attain escape velocity.

So did mine. No contractions like don't? The tell-tale pause before saying upset because no more precise emotional vocabulary was available? Or before establishing that the data needed to supply an exact number of days wasn't available, either? Her human voice had been dreamy and soft, but that uniform, cheap-robot tone, with the exact same spacing between each word, still shone through. It was a voice I hadn't heard her speak in since she got her first illegal personality. It was a voice she hated, but I loved.

"I mean with me," Trix said, uniformly emphatic.

Dared I hope that the natural, robo-raised

Trix from the welfare nursery was back to stay?

"All over me," Trix went on. "Inside and out."

Phys? I couldn't help worrying about AIDS 7. But her germ sensors would have screamed over that one. "That's great, Trix."

She touched her head and frowned.

"But your head still hurts?"

"It did not till I called you."

"Did you call that corp I told you about that fixes personality work damage? And did you call my current corp to get a contract so you'll have the yen to pay them?"

"Nan?"

"Yes?"

"Where did you get that British accent?"

"I'm still talking with it?"

"You had personality work?"

"'Course not, bot brain!"

Trix laughed, that funny mechanical laugh I'd almost forgotten.

I laughed with her, so happy to have the real Trix back.

"You know how much I love bot insults,"

she said, sounding, of course, just like a bot. "Revenge against all the flashing lights that raised me. So, Nan, it takes how many nanobots to—?"

"The true Trix, bad jokes and all!"

"Mart said I would do better at work without all that personality work and that anyway he wanted me to go natural. Is not he wonderful? There are just a few days I cannot account for. But I remember the time you phys pushed me into a fountain in Europe."

"One too many bot jokes."

"I remember my revenge!"

"What revenge? That pastry you slapped into my face was delicious." I was giddy, silly with happiness.

"Do not worry about my yen account. Wrap your little synchronous orbit around this: I am getting paid a galaxy to help supervise the aliens on their way home. So you better get that drive right, Nan."

My giddiness over Trix' recovery vanished. "But the drive—" I was going to say "only works one way" but I got that weird toe-moving feeling that first happened when I started talking like Lydia Bennet, and my throat clamped shut. Then I remembered that my drive would work just fine for a round trip.

"What is the matter, Nan? Your anger problem?"

"No, nothing, I just choked." My giddiness was back. I struck a theatrical pose, despite the toe-move feeling. "My brilliance is more than enough to get choked up about. What I was going to say is: But the drive is already all too perfect."

But Trix was looking elsewhere. "He stirs." She looked down. "In more ways than one." She winked, blew me a kiss, and was gone.

I grinned, laughed at the thought of actually, phys, sleeping with someone, stretched out to fully enjoy the bed I had all to myself, and dozed back off to sleep.

When I opened my eyes later that morning it occurred to me that I'd been so obsessed with the ship's drive that I hadn't left my house since the incident with the alien. Speaking of the alien...I waited at a part of the wall near where it had been working that day, curious to see how far it had gotten before it...starved? Phys contact was supposed to increase empathy, but it had had just the opposite effect on me. I could only tell myself that it had been a live, sentient being. I could more easily feel empathy for an antique steam engine that at least exhaled something I could understand.

The wall opened, and I stepped naked into the sunshine, again grateful that my closest neighbors were owls. I let the sun toast me, equally grateful for the genetic work that had eliminated skin cancer. Why had I been so obsessed with work lately that I'd denied myself this?

Tipping my face back, I raked my hair off my forehead as I walked so I could feel the warmth there. But it was, as always, useless. My hair did exactly what it wanted, springing right back.

Where the alien was supposed to have been working nothing had been done. I could empathize enough not to blame it. I took another step toward where I'd seen it last but stopped when I felt something odd underfoot. Kneeling down to sift through the dirt, I came up with a handful of long-dead worms. Puzzled, I stood, still holding them. Clumps of dirt were attached to each at one end. Apparently they'd been dead long enough to be hard, not squishy and wormlike at all, yet they were oddly pliable. And very long. And...

A large shadow passed overhead. Then another. I heard a deep, hollow hoot on one side of me, a loud wail on the other. The wind conspired against me when I looked up, helping my hair obscure my view, but I could see the snowy owl coming at me far faster than he ever had before. Then I was struck from behind, a sharp tear in the back of my neck pushing me toward the snowy I could see, who was swinging his legs forward as if he was going to land on my head. Instead he sank his claws into my skull. Flailing my arms, I dropped to the ground with both blood and hair obscuring my vision. But I could see there were two snowies circling back for another simultaneous attack, the second owl being the much-darker female. I scurried for the house, agonized as I waited for the wall to open. They pulled up short, back-pedaling with their massive wings. Alone I slid in across my floor amidst a cloud of feathers, hair and blood, screaming, "Walls, deny access."

But this breed's potential for aggression was unparalleled. Their first strikes against the outside walls were tentative; I suspected they thought the walls would make holes. Then came an endless and relentless pummeling, as if they expected to break in by sheer force of will. "Walls, clear vision 100%," I said. My lazy leaf pattern disappeared and there they were, diving at and crashing into my house from all sides. Just as I felt the telltale drip of something down my back, I spotted my blood smeared across the darker female's beak.

"Bitch!" I yelled.

She landed on the roof directly over my head and hissed, clawing my house. I jumped when the male, who could now see me as well as I could see him, smashed into the wall directly behind me at the same time that I heard a buzz in my ear.

"Son of a bitch!" I ran for my sim.

That Stupid Underling From Work.

Huh? It was, of course, the same voice that had woken me up in the middle of the night with Trix' call, but I didn't remember activating the command that would replace Reg's name with what I always called him. No matter. No time for it now. "Busy," I screeched, double pulling an earlobe that was sticky with blood.

I tried to print every kind of gun I could think of. My sim kept flashing, "Illegal print; cannot complete."

"Fucking Green Party," I spat, even though I always voted green.

Knife? Ax? Mag-powered saw? Inadequate, given the owls' speed and precision at close range versus my own. Fuck. But for every law there was always something no one thought of. I punched in "cross-bow."

Nothing. Then another deep, hollow hoot as the male slammed into the wall nearest me, but was I hearing something else underneath that racket?

Yes! My sim was printing! I reached out with both hands, wanting to at least touch my sim—cling to it, kiss it, perhaps—while it completed the print.

It was then that I noticed I was still clutching the dead worms, except that, with adrenaline ripping through my brain, I realized immediately that they weren't worms that were very long. They were very long tails...rats' tails. Must be the infamous Alaskan Nurat. The owls thought I was threatening their food source.

I looked up in time to see the female flying away, toward where I knew they raised their young.

The sim tray opened. I knew the nasty-looking thing I saw inside it would do the trick safely, from a distance. But I took the cross-bow out and tucked it behind my masterpiece, an elephant it had taken me a year to carve from sim wood.

The male was circling for another attack but looking tired now. I looked again at the

rat tails I'd had in my hand and returned to
my sim.

I punched in "Alaskan Nurat."

My sim quickly printed a picture. Some
dumb text at the side was going on about how
the only rats in Alaska used to be on an island
called, appropriately, Rat Island.

I punched in "Alaskan Nurat, real."

My sim flashed a question mark, then
apparently thought better of it. It printed a
roasted rat in a disgusting-smelling sauce I
didn't think either I, or an owl, could tolerate.
I counted the tails I'd been holding: six. I
punched in "twelve whole, dead Alaskan
Nurats, raw and plain."

Good as my sim was, I suspected a true
connoisseur, and that certainly included the
snowies, could tell the difference. Still I
carried the twelve dead rats, and the six tails,
to the wall. "Walls, access for me only."

There was a tired thump above my head.
While he was circling, which was now taking
longer and longer, was as good a time as any.
I took a deep breath and stepped close
enough to the wall to prompt it to make an

opening.

The snowy landed on the ground nearby, looking exhausted. I suspected the blood on his face was his own. He was just trying to take care of his family.

From inside my house I stretched out both hands in his direction, holding a dead rat in each. I carefully placed them on the ground, then put the other ten there, too. I even added the six tails. Then I rocked back on my heels, far enough for the wall to close. I figured not seeing each other might further defuse the situation. "Walls, close vision 100%."

I was sunk into pitch black but gratified to hear scratching outside where I'd left my offering.

Buzz.

What now?

That Stupid Underling From Work.

Reg again.

"Light, 40%." I double-pulled my ear. "Ten-second notice." Nine. I scrambled to my feet. Eight. Seven. I used my sheets to wipe the blood off my forehead. Six. I let my

hair flop forward since I was still bleeding a
little. Five. I remembered I was naked. Four.
I spotted a long shirt I'd left on the floor.
Three. Two. I got it over my head. One. I
plastered on a smile.

I knew Rococo was in style and had talked
to Reg before, but still... I was no longer
infuriated but at least amused to see an
apparition out of David Copperfield invade
my house. Except Reg's matching eyes and
hair were copper-colored, giving him a glitter
he didn't otherwise possess. Unless you
wanted to count the Mr. Micawber-esque
brocade vest that his pot belly displayed to full
advantage.

I managed an out-of-breath, "Good
morning."

"Is it night there? It seems so dark. Did I
wake you? Maybe you're not on Universal
Time?"

I mumbled, "Light, 50%."

"Maybe it's this stupid phone. I tried to
get it reprogrammed last year, but they said
they'd have to operate, digging rather deep,
and—"

"Light, 70%."

"Oh there, I can see you very well now. My, my, my, but I didn't realize dresses were getting shorter again, especially that short."

"Light, 60%."

"Hmmm. That's funny. Your lighting keeps changing. Must be this damn phone again. Maybe I should get it swapped out phys after all. What's one more deep implant surgery at this point, right? Or wrong. What do you think?"

"Any chance of swapping out that brain?"

"Funny, I don't remember your having an accent. What is it? Old Aussie or something? You know I always think those old vids with everyone talking differently are so much fun. But I didn't quite catch what you said. The accent and you're mumbling."

I spoke louder. "And I didn't quite catch why you're calling."

"Why I'm calling? Why I'm calling. Oh. That. Did our boss ever call you?"

"No."

"Funny. He said he was going to, like I told you last time we spoke, and since then he seems to have disappeared."

"So, you called because you're trying to locate a typically mysterious corp boss?"

"How can I possibly get my contract renewed if I can't get a response from him? How in the solar system am I supposed to come up with the yen to get a new phone implant if—"

He hadn't even been looking at me when I hung up on him. With any luck when he finally noticed he'd blame his phone. Real people. So deeply flawed. Why put up with them when even a third-rate sex site could faux phys someone far more logical, consistent, and better suited to my tastes?

Quiet. Blessed quiet. Only occasional scratching outside around my rat peace-offering.

"Light, 80%." It might only have been a silly dream, but I'd been left with a profound unease about my star drive. Time to get back to my recent toe-tingling obsession with work.

Buzz.

Damn.

That Stupid Underling From Work.

Enough Rococo. Double pulling it, I almost yanked my earlobe off. "Busy." All that early 21st century corp privacy-protection legislation? And Reg really thought I could help him locate an American corp boss who apparently didn't want to be located?

"Screen, last." My work popped up in front of me in 3D. I started dragging and dropping, crunching and re-crunching numbers, plotting trajectories.

Find our boss? I'd barely found the scandal when he'd had a contract with a previous corp. Accused of ordering a malfunction in gameware that killed some TexMexes. Cleared when the R&D guy who developed the gameware reversed his testimony. But I couldn't shake the feeling that I was working for an ancient, and thoroughly disreputable, traveling circus.

"Screen, refresh." Convenient that the aliens' planet was between us and the galaxy's core, since my star drive would be tethered to the pull from its black hole, through the dark matter and energy that made up most of the universe. Still, there it was again: no way to return. It was obvious every time I reviewed the data, and what I would have told the boss, if he'd ever called. But more than that toe-tingling obsession with work, I now felt that odd toe-moving sensation. That's right; not a problem. The ship's drive would work perfectly in both directions. I'd broken through the myth of inherently impractical interstellar exploration! I'd thought I'd have to be resurrected from my cryopreserved grave to see that.

Yet something kept nagging me, perhaps just a silly leftover from my dreams.

"Screen, match drive capacity to exact payload." I knew we were taking only the relatively few, still-healthy aliens. Maybe it was that discrepancy in the food supplies I'd noted. I settled into my favorite papasan chair for the long haul. But I knew reviewing long lists in search of the missing rations for the aliens wouldn't keep me awake long.

"Thank you."

Where the fuck did that come from? It wasn't my phone, it wasn't the house, and it most certainly wasn't me. True, I'd dozed off, for awhile since my screen had disappeared, but I was positive it wasn't from a dream, either. All I had was a slowly settling sense of where it came from—directly over my head, just above my house—and that weird toe-move feeling. I bolted to the nearest wall and waited for it to make a hole.

"Thank you" was only my mind's reflexive translation. What had come from just above my house was a maelstrom of harsh impulses, none expressed, or even felt, in words: Lust, from the male perspective. Hunger with an unquenchable desire to crush something with the mouth, feeling it struggle, then tasting its blood. Unflinching perseverance. But what had risen for one brief moment above all these was gratitude.

The wall opened. Only then did I remember the incidents of the morning and notice my rat offerings were gone. I looked up just in time to see the snowy soaring toward their nest with the last rat. Trajectory. Velocity. I didn't have to call up my screen to know what had been directly over my head.

"You're welcome," I called after the

snowy, scratching my head. Then I stepped back into my house, seriously cleaning up and letting the gadgetry in my bathroom tend my wounds before getting dressed. Why had I been so obsessed with work lately that I seemed to forget about all else?

Almost finished with the star drive, I wondered what else I could design to entertain the idle rich.

"Screen, current star drive, ship, human passengers." Meter-high, 3D, full-body stills turned in front of me. I'd never seen so many people trying to bring back the glory of ancient Spain. Women wore long skirts that stuck out at the sides. Wearing ceremonial swords, men showed their legs off with tights...whether or not they were worth showing off. I smiled.

Toe tingling and toe moving. Why wasn't I just hurrying to complete my work and ignoring those rich, snobby Tex-Mex Nucastilians? Did I really want them not only taking Texas back but going after Arizona and Numexico, too? In this global world had patriotism gone completely out of style? Yes,

I wanted to convince the TexMexes that my star drive would give them a perfect, trouble-free round trip. But what I really wanted was their deaths.

That toe-moving feeling. Where was all this shit, including the British accent, coming from? Those weren't my feelings about the TexMexes. Those weren't even my words.

A cold shiver went up my spine. No, not possible. How could I have gotten genetic work done without ever having left home? It had to be new side effects from all the reputable therapies I'd gotten from Sachs for my anger problem. Then it hit me: my daily anger problem was gone. That should have made me insanely happy; oddly, it sent another shiver up my spine.

Toes... I had to finish my work quickly on that drive. And something about a hat. No, not a hat. A bonnet.

No therapy I agreed to, or even combination of therapies, could put Lydia Bennet's bonnets into my head or let me hear what an owl was thinking. I'd been ignoring a whole lot of new shit I never ordered.

I pulled my earlobe. "Trix."

Audio first: "—to stop. You and Nan have to meet each other." I was again relieved to hear Trix' natural, robotically uniform cadence.

Some guy's voice: "But of course. Forgive my selfishness. I'm just so in love. You, Trix, are a beautiful woman."

And there they were, all cuddled up in bed together, cute as could be. Silly grins on the both of them. Even a staunch porn-site fan such as myself had to grin with them.

"Trix," I said, "I'm so sorry to interrupt."

"Anger problem...upsetting you?" Trix looked concerned.

"Someone with consummate good taste," said the guy, "must have picked out that accent."

"Thanks," I told the guy, "but that, not anger, is my problem. Trix, remember how we were kidding around last time we spoke about the accent meaning I must have gotten personality work?"

Even the guy looked concerned, darting a quick look at Trix.

"Don't worry about a thing, you two. But, Trix, I need to ask you one thing."

"Sure."

"When you get a new personality do you ever get an odd feeling, for me it's like a toe— Well, never mind that. Just tell me, do you get an odd feeling when a genetically actuated personality kicks in with things that aren't naturally you?"

Now the guy—Mart, if I remembered correctly—was tickling Trix under the sheets.

"Stop!" she directed his way, though none too convincingly. "I am so glad it is not your anger problem," she said to me between bursts of giggles. "Stop! Really! Let me think!" Finally, "Yes. For me it is a little like— Stop! I mean it! Like the first time I positioned my mouth correctly and got a flute to play. Why?"

"Nothing," I said, reaching for my earlobe, but pausing before ending the call to blow them a kiss. "Sweet dreams, you two."

Despite the chill going up my spine over Trix' first with the flute, like my first with that toe, I had to smile at the sweetness of what I'd just seen. Even if, thinking about the guy, of all eye colors, I really was not into magenta.

But I found myself scowling, amidst a new outbreak of that toe-moving feeling, at the 3-D stills of the TexMexes I'd left twirling about in mid-air. Had patriotism gone completely out of style? All their power and influence. I'd been unnaturally obsessed with their damn star drive, ignoring everything that was wrong with me to get it finished. My toes almost hurt. What the fuck had those snobby Nucastilians done to me?

I tried to shake my feelings off. But who else could it have been? They had technology we didn't. Maybe this bizarre wish to see them dead meant my subconscious knew something I didn't. I'd been working on their drive at many times my usual speed. Jupiter's failed star, who else stood to benefit from infecting me with that obsession?

Like some old holo noir, they must have done it while I slept so obviously wouldn't tell me. But if I made up some excuse to talk with them, maybe I could pick up some useful information.

The only help available for illegal personality work was the corp I'd researched on Trix' behalf. But they wouldn't see anyone unless the symptoms were constant, not intermittent like mine. What else could I do? Contact the authorities about the ill effects of personality work I could be arrested for?

Judging from their stats, I couldn't find any reason to call one TexMex rather than another. So I pulled my earlobe and called the guy whose tights showed off a truly great pair of legs.

Again I was sunk into pitch black as my house went dead. A recorded announcement told me this was because I had reached the secure line of someone who only communicated in dead rooms, phys. I was to state my name and business to see if I would be "granted an audience."

Shit.

But my corp's boss hadn't called, couldn't be reached and—as was traditional—I didn't even have his name. Somehow I had to find out things "that stupid underling from work" wouldn't know.

I stated my name. Business? What would get me an audience? I said it was about the star drive I'd already tested by launching a prototype from the moon, and that we were well into construction of the ship there, only awaiting a few final specs. Then, very quickly in the hope I wouldn't trip myself up, I lied. For some reason the toe-moving feeling went crazy, though for some other reason I didn't understand either, it didn't completely feel like a lie. I had said there was a real problem with the star drive.

If someone told me there was a "real problem" with my ship's interstellar drive, I'd "grant an audience." I waited in the darkness.

Audience granted. Same day. I was told to punch "Lexington, TexMex" into the mag car I hadn't even ordered yet, but I was pretty sure there wasn't a real city called Lexington in either the old Mexico or the new TexMex that included Texas. Or the entire American Southwest.

The recording finished the call by telling me I was now under surveillance by the TexMex government, and that any mention of this location or my appointment there, or a failure to keep that appointment, could lead to serious consequences.

Maybe I should have started my investigation with that disreputable circus I was working for.

My house crackled back to life. I pulled my earlobe. "That Stupid Underling From Work."

"—the sim on the left in the cafeteria, not the one on the right. I don't care what you tell me, food from the one on the right always tastes more acidic, and I have very sensitive dental implants. And please be quick about it, I'm—" He stopped when he saw me. "What are you doing here? And where's the short skirt?"

"Apparently you answered your phone," I said. Under TexMex surveillance? Should be careful, but I was on a fishing expedition anyway; I hardly knew what to ask this idiot.

"Oh... Is that what that buzz was? The one just before I had to scratch my ear?" He was scratching his copper hair, apparently struggling with the logistics of answering a phone.

I wondered if he'd required, at some point in his life, instructions on breathing.

"I liked that short skirt."

"Thanks," I managed without choking. "Have you heard from the boss? Curious, since you told me last week he was going to call me, but he never did."

"The boss?"

"Of our corp."

"Oh. Him."

"I've been doing a lot of work on the star drive," I said. "Almost finished. I'm not quite ready but I want to be sure the boss isn't going to add an extra spec before I sign off on the damn thing."

"You got the original specs I sent you on his behalf?"

"Yes."

"Then we're set. Didn't want my contract voided. Or the boss'. Or yours. Or your twitchy friend Trix'."

"She told you we're friends?"

"No, she no longer speaks to any..." Suddenly his copper irises glittered brightly, and he trailed off. He looked scared then, but finally continued. "I mean, yes, of course."

Huh? Seemed like he'd just lied to me, but why?

His food arrived, commanding his full attention. He spilled most of his first bite onto the brocade vest his belly thrust forward to make such a thing easier.

What was that lie about? One thing, sadly, was certain: No one would tell this idiot any more confidential information than they had to. Still, he was all I had.

"Reg, what do you know about our clients, the TexMexes?"

"They should all die."

Surprise popped my eyes wide. Had they done something to him, too?

"But we mustn't tell them that."

Brilliant. Bear-trap mind.

"Anything else you need to know?" Reg asked.

"Tell me everything you know about the TexMexes on our passenger list. It will help me." I knew what I was opening myself up to. I only hoped I'd have enough time before leaving for "Lexington, TexMex" to pan even one useful piece of information out of the onslaught of useless sludge to come.

Toes tingling, I quietly called up my screen so it was only visible to me. I hoped Reg wouldn't notice when I dragged and dropped it over his eyes, so I could at least get some work done while he chattered. Then I shrunk my visible range and used a control pad so I wouldn't continue to do anything with my hands that he could see.

Predictably, he reacted with, "You're really loving all their recipes I'm sharing with you, aren't you?"

"Fascinating."

"So this one that's high up in their government—let's see if I can get his full name out—Sancho Diego Jose Francisco de Panza Juan Cipriano de la Castilla."

The guy with the great legs I was going to see.

"Your jaw dropped. What's he mean to you?"

"Nothing," I lied. But I added with real sincerity, "I just want to congratulate you on managing to get that name out of your mouth."

"The boss... Well, never mind."

Aha. I closed my screen. "The boss...had you memorize that name, didn't he?"

"How'd you know?"

"Well it's so obvious. I mean, come on." I laughed, totally lost but banking on his stupidity to buy that I was a friendly comrade in on all our corp's secrets, too.

"He told you, too? In those specs?"

"Of course. I'm working on the damn star drive, aren't I?"

"That's true. So what do you think?"

"I think...it's what we've got to do."

Reg stared at me in silence.

I crossed my fingers out of his visual range, hoping against hope that I hadn't at last knocked myself out of orbit by saying the wrong thing. But a vice grip in the pit of my stomach said I had. And besides, even Reg should be able to figure out that no one would have put a confidential secret in the specs. I just hoped he wouldn't figure that out till after he spilled something that might help me in "Lexington, TexMex."

Reg continued to stare, then he did a very odd thing: he started to blink back tears. "Are you sure we have to do it?"

"What choice do we have?" I tried to sound sympathetic.

He was losing the battle with his tears. He bit his lip, and snuffled loudly.

Jupiter's failed star, I wished I knew what we were talking about. I stole a look at my masterpiece, my sim-wood elephant. I'd carved an extra fold in one ear that housed an old-fashioned, phys, timepiece. I only had minutes before I had to rent the mag car.

Reg leaned in real close, cutting his nose off by exceeding his projection range. "There's something I bet you don't know." But then he stopped, looked sharply sideways, and leaned back. "Thanks, it wasn't too bad."

"What's wrong with your eyes?" asked someone I couldn't see.

"My eyes? Oh. I did react to the basil in the pesto. You know I've told you about my allergies."

Not a bad cover at all! Looked like I'd

have to revise my opinion of Reg.

"Nan, I've gotta go." He ended the call.

Damn! I looked into my elephant's ear again. But no time to cry about it. I yanked my ear and ordered the mag car, having to settle for some third-rate corp I'd never heard of since they were the only ones with a car immediately available nearby. Food. I printed Coca Cola's beef stew. Okay, I was getting sick of it by now, but this was no time to find my next food fad, and it smelled better than roasted rat. My hair. Going formal, I raked my fingers through it as I waited for the nearest wall to make a hole for me. My hair, of course, immediately fell back into its original, natural position: sticking out in all directions. The hole opened. I stepped outside, slugging down some beef stew as I did so. I tried not to spill like Reg had, though my simple at-home-wear in no way mimicked his brocade vest. Not at all Rococo, I was wearing a blue tunic and matching, loose-legged capris...first printed for practicing martial arts. Hardly ideal for my meeting with Nucastilian "royalty," but there'd been no time to change.

Where was the damn mag car? "Walls, clear vision 100%," I said, squinting past all my stuff inside to find it hovering over my garden on the exact opposite end of my house. The closer I got, the more convinced I was it belonged in a museum. Flying glass tire, minus the hole. I wasn't sure what came first: that design or the room-temperature superconductor. Close up, I could see not only dents in the gray stuff housing the superconductor on the bottom, but that a small piece was actually torn away from the edge of the glass and hanging free. Silly thing couldn't even ID me to open the door till I almost knocked into it.

Inside I took special care to check that what I could see or feel of the chassis was solid, that my seat was securely anchored, and that I wrapped myself with twice as much safety netting as usual before punching in "Lexington, TexMex."

I was plunged into darkness as all the glass went black. Of course. TexMex security. I should have foreseen that one. So much for enjoying the view.

Slowly my eyes adjusted to what this antique deemed adequate interior light. I could hear the wind outside and what I guessed were my silver tulips scraping against the bottom, hopefully not getting hurt by that little piece hanging off. Then I heard the hiss of carbon dioxide jets steering the thing as it executed a dizzying about face, fast enough for that hanging piece to decapitate my tulips, followed by a klutzy leap forward.

Nothing for it but to question my sanity for this whole idea and shovel down the rest of my stew. Just as I finished, I felt a telltale climb upwards. I scrambled to check the door seals, fortunately all secure, as we entered the vacuum of the Alaska-California elevated tube.

It was then that I picked up movement in my peripheral vision and looked down. Odd. Though enclosed in a totally blacked-out car, compliments of TexMex paranoia, with no holo enhancements activated, I was seeing a constantly changing kaleidoscope of patterns flowing over a sliver of the rounded floor.

Funny, they kind of reminded me of—

I ripped myself out of the safety netting and twisted myself around till I was almost upside down, face pressed up against the glass at the bottom of the rounded floor.

Tube ads. I'd have recognized their frenetic pace anywhere. What TexMex security failed to factor in, when correctly blacking out the windows of this particular model, was the tiny place at the bottom where the piece hanging off had left more glass exposed than usual. I couldn't see much, but I could see out. Still, no point standing upside down to watch ads in an enclosed tube.

I righted and re-webbed myself. What was my plan? Uh, excuse me, Sancho, but can you tell me what in the solar system your government did to me? And why—other than my faith it would work and my obsession to get the work done—you would mess around with a person developing a star drive your life will depend on?

Motivation. I had to worry not only about figuring out what their motivation was, but I also had to somehow motivate them to tell me what they obviously had no intention of telling me. How could I make it worth their while to tell me what they'd done to me? Convince them that the accuracy of my work and judgment was being impaired?

I fidgeted; the webbing made its usual odd, crunchy sound. A hypnotic kaleidoscope of patterns danced over that sliver of floor, the ads' intermittent rhythm reminiscent of many a sleepy ride south.

Intermittent. Except for the British accent, I'd managed to ignore my symptoms because, like elusive mechanical problems, they were intermittent. I wasn't always Lydia Bennet, unlike Trix who'd been 100% any of her personalities. Even the corp I'd researched to help Trix stated that genetic personality work was constant. Was mine intermittent because, unlike Trix' phys work, the work on me had been done remotely? Or was it just that, as my Grandpa O used to always say with a huge grin, I was stubborn as hell.

The car was slowing. Felt a little too soon for the TexMex border. I yanked the webbing off again and did another half headstand, banging my head wound from the snowy attack against the floor when the car took the telltale dive onto an exit ramp.

I could see daylight, typical southwestern terrain. Could have been anywhere. Then I saw it. I might not be able to tell the difference between Phoenix, Arizona, and Nogales in TexMex, but I sure as hell knew when I was looking at the Grand Canyon. Had someone violated national landmark status by installing superconductors down the sides of—?

Hoped so as I fell over the cliff's edge, then banged my face against the glass as the car descended down the side of the canyon. But it was at a controlled speed. How could anyone have installed— More to the point, where was I going?

All I could see was rock. The ride was jerky enough from the uneven surface, even if the car hovered above it, that my forearms were getting tired from bracing myself in my awkward position. But at last I got a glimpse of water which could only mean I'd reached the bottom.

There was a thunderously loud sound in front of the car where I couldn't see. The car moved forward slowly as the daylight dimmed and finally darkened altogether when I heard the thunderously loud sound behind me.

A door. I rushed to right and re-web myself. Revealing that I knew where I was might not be wise if the mag car door opened to reveal some TexMex customs official, checking me before I continued in what I assumed was a secret tunnel leading to TexMex.

The mag car's glass cleared. Before I could orient myself, its door burst open and, despite the webbing, someone snatched me out, spat in my face, and sent me sprawling across a hard stone floor. I slid to a stop in front of a pair of legs I would have recognized anywhere. Sancho.

Behind me a voice bellowed, "Murder no more Castilian royalty, American peasant."

I sprang to my feet. "What in the solar system are you talking about?"

The man who'd snatched me out of the

car, like Sancho, was wearing tights. But with his chubby legs it was a mistake. He was trying to answer me but so beside himself with fury that he couldn't get the words out.

We were in a bunker of some kind. I took a deep draught of its dank air and crouched defensively. Then I wiped his spit off my face. Insanely, I almost smiled as my hand passed before my nose, thinking of my Grandpa O. The spit smelled of tobacco.

Chubby Legs waved his hands about impatiently, working invisible controls. "Refresh your memory." His voice oozed sarcasm. With a sneer he snapped his fingers and then pointed a contemptuous index finger in front of my face.

A projection appeared in front of me. In the holo I again saw Reg spill most of his first bite onto his brocade vest. It took me awhile to get it, especially since I was distracted by Chubby Legs who, behind the holo, was stalking me like a lion. But then I watched myself say, "I think...it's what we've got to do." And then, "What choice do we have?"

Sancho spoke for the first time: "At least

that pig had the cojones to question, and to weep." It was a beautiful voice, deep and rich like the ancient mahogany of Grandpa O's elaborately carved desk.

Chubby Legs pounced. I wasn't fool enough to pit my upper body strength against a hefty man, but I'd been comparing our heights. I thought I could defend by dropping into a marriage of a Capoeira Esquiva and a classic Chuck-Norris drop kick, but the man was faster than I'd anticipated for anyone that plump. He grabbed my ankle before my foot hit his "cojones." I just barely pivoted my body in time for the inevitable hard twist to my ankle or it would have been my head that hit that stone floor. As he dragged me back to my feet by the scruff of my neck I wanted to believe I at least saw a moment of respect for trying in Sancho's eyes.

Chubby twisted my arm hard against my back, which he pinned against him. The smell of tobacco on his breath brought no hint of a smile this time. "Meet the wife and kids." Again the finger snap and point in front of my face.

"Not again, Miguel." Raw pain cut through Sancho's voice. "I beg you. Not for her sake, but for yours."

At first I didn't understand the projection Miguel dragged and dropped, almost on my nose. It was hard to focus on that close.

Some meat dish the wife prepared particularly well? Then my brain made the necessary adjustments and the holo snapped into focus. No, that was the wife. A large part of her skull was missing. She was holding what was left of two kids.

"Observe the consequences of a 'minor little gameware scandal.' Compliments of your current 'boss.' Being an American peasant, you don't even know his name."

Mercifully I was blinded by my tears.

Miguel's anger was as nothing compared to the icy cold that came next. "Tell us exactly what you laughingly told Reg you know all about, since you're working on the star drive. How much time you waste telling us you know nothing will decide how many teeth, fingers, and eyes you lose."

My eyes widened, clearing enough tears

for me to see that I was positioned perfectly to stomp hard on Miguel's instep. But, stupid as it was, I couldn't look at what was left of his family and hurt him more, no matter what he was about to do to me. Besides, my stomach—

I splattered a full serving of Coca Cola's beef stew all over the cold stone floor. Next I was overcome by convulsions I didn't understand until I remembered what it was like to really cry, the kind of crying I hadn't done since I was a kid. Was it for Miguel, for his family, or out of fear of what Miguel was going to do to me? Maybe all three.

I heard a sniff from Miguel behind me, and saw Sancho's eyes were moist. My survival instincts roared back to the surface.

"Do you think I could fake all this?" I choked out between sobs and dry heaves. "Look again at my phone call with Reg, because I was faking that." I choked back some stomach bile. "Look at my eyes when he surprised me by saying you should all die. Listen to my awkward laugh and stilted speech, saying nothing, because I don't know what I'm talking about!"

Miguel paid no attention, twisting the arm he held behind my back more. The pain was unbearable, but I couldn't blame him any more than I could blame the snowies for attacking when they thought I was stealing their family's food supply.

Sancho? At first I despaired, watching his angular face tighten. Then I realized how much effort he was putting into that stoniness. But he started to turn away, as if he might leave me with Miguel.

Desperate, I hurried on. "And look at my face when Reg ended the call and I didn't have to conceal my disappointment because I'd failed to get any information from him."

"Shut up," spat Miguel.

But Sancho started to review a small holo of the phone call.

"Who arranged for us to meet today? Who alerted you to a problem with the star drive?" I pleaded, wondering what problem I was going to have to make up amidst a new attack of that toe-moving feeling.

Miguel let up a little of the pressure on my

arm.

But Sancho was suddenly on top of us, his hand a vice grip holding my face. "What exactly is wrong with the star drive, American peasant?"

Sancho's fingers dug into my neck; I started to black out. Then more of that odd toe-moving feeling: I "heard" the words "todos suenan lo que son, aunque ninguno lo entiende" in my head, though I had no idea what they meant. Sancho loosened his grip.

Time to lie. "The problem with the star drive is—" That toe-moving feeling, so strong this time it hurt: "I wish you joy. If you love Mr. Darcy half as well as I do my dear Wickham, you must be very happy. It is a great comfort to have you so rich, and when you have nothing else to do, I hope you will think of us. I am sure Wickham would like a place at court very much, and I do not think we shall have quite money enough to live upon without some help. Any place would do, of about three or four hundred a year..."

Both Sancho and Miguel released me. I thought them stupid, disagreeable fellows, and

I told them stoutly, "I am not afraid; for though I am the youngest, I'm the tallest."

They each backed away a few steps. I thought them rather rude and impertinent. "I suppose you will bid me hold my tongue, but I would bid you hold yours, especially when you say things like 'todos suenan lo que son, aunque ninguno lo entiende' that I do not in the least understand."

Sancho stopped dead in his tracks, his eyes as big as saucers. But what was a saucer? I frowned.

Miguel spoke to Sancho, as if I wasn't there. "Tell me, since when does an American peasant know Calderon de la Barca's poetry?"

"I doubt she does," Sancho answered. "But what she just recited perfectly are the exact lines that just popped into my head: 'everyone dreams what they are but nobody understands.'"

"Correct me if I'm wrong, but I didn't hear you say that, in either language," Miguel said.

"That's the point, Miguel. I didn't say it aloud."

"Know what else is strange? That British accent."

"I know. It isn't accurate."

Miguel snapped his fingers and pointed in front of me, only because I stood between them. Really, the whole sordid business was getting tremendously tiresome, and I quite suspected it was time for tea.

A holo of myself appeared, in a progress report I'd made for the TexMexes long ago. No British accent. Then Miguel waved it aside and replaced it with my last conversation with Reg.

"The vowels are accurate," Sancho mused, "but that accent omits the consonant 'r' and she's pronouncing every 'r.'"

"Watch this." Miguel waved my phone call aside. He replaced it with news coverage of the R&D guy's testimony accusing my boss of ordering a malfunction in gameware that killed Miguel's family. No British accent. Miguel waved that aside and replaced it with news coverage of the same R&D guy reversing his testimony. British accent, but inaccurate. He was pronouncing every "r."

Suddenly I wasn't thinking about tea. Why the fuck should I? I never drank tea. It was as if I was roused from some odd, waking dream.

My inaccurate British accent was apparently constant. But the intermittent bouts of being Jane Austen's immortal airhead from *Pride and Prejudice*, Lydia Bennet? Never before had such a bout been so severe.

Maybe the R&D guy could help me, whereas the TexMexes, obviously as befuddled as I was, could not. Whatever had happened to me had happened to the R&D guy, as well. Arms free, I yanked my earlobe and said his name.

Nothing happened. Of course.

Sancho turned to me, studying me carefully. "Even if we allowed you to make calls, that one would do you no good."

Miguel snapped his fingers and pointed in front of me. More news coverage. But TexMex, in Spanish. Still I could read the recent date off a banner, and I didn't need a translator to know I was looking at the partially decomposed body of the R&D guy.

"Stabbed and strangled," said Sancho. "Hidden in a holo rug in a remote location. If it hadn't been for a power outage temporarily disrupting the holography, the satellite would never have spotted the corpse."

Miguel added, "Notice the story was suppressed in the Stolen States of America. With your laws protecting confidentiality, we didn't even know the gameware corp's boss was the same as yours till after we ordered the starship."

But I was still thinking about the accent he'd shared with me. Something was tickling the back of my mind. Who did I talk to recently who liked my British accent? Reg? No, he'd just liked what he thought was my short skirt.

Sancho and Miguel's looked-like-real-leather boots clattered across the stone as they withdrew to talk among themselves in Spanish, while casting me sideways glances and fingering their ceremonial swords. All I could hear were questions including my name and the word "confianza," and something about "verdad la maquina."

Should I run? Where to? We were enclosed in a huge cave, outside a building carved from stone. Soldiers, dressed like conquistadors, surrounded my mag car. I doubted I could get the cave door re-opened.

A real, phys dog crossed in front of me, tits hanging from her belly and swinging as she walked.

A woman emerged from the building, her skirt long but not wide. I smiled approvingly at her clothes' simplicity, until she used a strip of white cloth in the front to scoop up my vomit.

"That's my mess. And besides, don't you have any bots?"

She smiled up at me. Obviously she hadn't understood a word.

I heard the clatter of approaching boots. Desperate I snatched the cloth out of her hand. "If anybody's going to do that it should be me."

Sancho reached us first. "A woman's purpose is to please, but she is also a woman." He handed the cloth back, which was still tied to her waist, and pulled me to my feet. A memory of old vid stirred, and I finally pieced it together: a servant in an apron.

Sancho gestured toward the house with a flourish, then took one of my hands, squeezing it into the crook of his elbow. "This way, señorita."

Better than being tossed across the floor. I luxuriated till it occurred to me that, like my phone, my germ sensors might not be working.

Inside everything was also phys: stone and black metal twisted into elaborate designs. Sancho seated me next to a huge, rough-hewn—was it possible?—real wood table. Covered with gadgetry like Grandpa O used to make.

A huge map of the United States, labeled "Robado Estados de America," adorned one wall. As far as I could tell from the Spanish, all the state names had been replaced by the names of the countries that had owned that land before we did. A picture of a man nearby was labeled "Juan Cortina." Another was labeled "Remember the Alamo," except the building had been crossed out and a picture of some land surrounded by water on three sides replaced it. The word Alamo had been crossed out and replaced with "San Jacinto."

Sancho bellowed something in Spanish, and another servant appeared with something for me to drink, which she told me in broken English would settle my stomach.

Miguel hooked me up to one of the gadgets he kept referring to as a "verdad la maquina," wrapping straps around my forehead, wrists and ankles. Mouth dry, I guzzled the drink.

Mistake.

It did relax my stomach beautifully, but it tasted funny and suddenly I couldn't keep my eyes open. I felt Sancho shoving soft things against different sides of me as my flaccid muscles threatened to tip me onto the floor, first in one direction, then another. My eyes fluttered. Miguel adjusted the straps of what I took to be some kind of lie detector. At least they were trying something other than removing body parts. My eyes closed completely.

Grandpa O. He was standing in front of me, the wind whipping his hair about smartly. But there was something wrong. He said he was emigrating to Mars. And I felt something I *couldn't possibly* feel about my beloved Grandpa O...volcanic eruptions of completely irrational *anger*. My eyes fluttered open.

Sancho's face was where Grandpa O's had been. "He was wise to emigrate," said Sancho, with a wry smile. Had I spoken aloud? My eyes closed again.

I was looking at an old pipe and a red ball. Filled with hate, I swept them off the table with such a violent gesture that I hurt my arm.

My eyes opened to find Sancho cradling my arm, then closed again.

Grandpa O, giving me the old pipe and the red ball. But something was wrong: no Teddy Roosevelt grin. My Grandpa O always had a Teddy Roosevelt grin. Then I could feel myself saying his words along with him, "Are you sure, Nan?" And I could feel myself saying my words aloud, too, "Why would I go to Mars with you?"

"Because there's nothing human left on Earth."

"Why are you giving me your stinky old pipe and that ratty red ball?"

"Remember when you were little, Nan? When I taught you about the solar system, using this ball for Mars? You're mad at me now, but maybe someday..." I stopped saying his words as I watched him pause to regain control of himself. "You'll find these two things in an old box somewhere, think of all the time we had together, and smile." And there it was again, the Teddy Roosevelt grin.

"I can't ever be mad at you, my precious Grandpa of Oz."

His words hurt in my throat. "Even when we're no longer together?"

My words cut me like knives. "Even then. I promise. Whatever I get mad at for the rest of my life, it won't be you."

Far, far away I heard Miguel's words, distorted as if they were coming through water. He was asking me something about a ship's drive I'd designed, but I hadn't yet done any such thing. I was fresh out of school.

Finally my eyes opened, but I wasn't really conscious.

Watching me, Sancho's dark eyes were moist. Then I had that odd feeling in my toe, and I was hearing Spanish again, but Sancho's mouth wasn't moving like Miguel's was, and Miguel was speaking in English.

Of course I couldn't understand the Spanish, but then other things came along with the words. At first it was just a hint of non-verbal feelings, like those I'd "heard" from the snowy, slowly getting stronger and stronger. Then my eyes fluttered closed again and there were images.

The face of a beautiful but ancient woman hovered where Grandpa O's face had been. She looked like Sancho, same regally sculpted face, same high, sweeping eyebrows. But her eyes were closed. Then the feelings soared, the exact anguish I felt when my Grandpa O left me on the last ship to Mars. Next I realized why the woman's eyes were closed. She was surrounded by white satin and real wood. She was laid out in a coffin.

His pain was unbearable. My eyes opened

wide. Both of my hands were straining against the straps attached to my wrists so I could tenderly caress Sancho's face.

"Su dulce abuela," I said. "Your sweet grandmother was dead. You couldn't even hope against hope that she would somehow— on a comet, on a meteor, on something crazy she made in the backyard that she had to kick to keep going—come back home to you from Mars."

"Your wrists," said Sancho, pulling my hands away from his face gently and rubbing them where the straps had left red marks. Finally he bent over them to kiss my hands. It was a strange feeling, another person touching me so.

"Recognize the telepathy?" Miguel spat, coming closer. "After all the money our government spent developing it, those American peasants perfected it first?"

But my eyes were closing again, my hands falling into the warm cavities of Sancho's hands holding them, my fingers intermingling with his. I thought of his grandmother and, before my muscles were again totally limp, squeezed his hands. He squeezed back. In a haze, as my consciousness spiraled downward, I was no longer sure which fingers were mine and which were Sancho's, but it no longer seemed to matter. My eyes shut tight.

Miguel's voice, closer, asked me about the star drive again. The straps tightened around my sore wrists like blood pressure cuffs and, I realized, around my ankles and forehead, too.

The star drive. Something about the star drive. Something...wrong. Something terribly wrong. "It's," I started to say, "it's..."

Miguel's voice, still sounding underwater but even closer. "Tell us, American peasant. It's what?" His question crashed against my eardrums like a tidal wave.

The answer roared back through my brain like a tsunami: All those damn sails and scoops? If big enough to collect adequate fuel from the near vacuum of space, they're big enough to feel drag from that same fuel that makes space a near, not a complete, vacuum. All admittedly convincing arguments to the contrary collapsed when the first microscopic prototypes approached the speed of light.

The only way I can get you to the stars is by tethering you to the black hole at the center of the Milky Way, through the dark matter and energy that makes up over 95% of the known universe.

Theoretically it should be reversible. It should work in both directions, not unlike tacking with the sails of an ancient sailing ship. But, though the prototypes I tested shot away from the moon, they never returned. Again, despite admittedly convincing arguments to the contrary, my drive can only provide adequate thrust if you're headed toward the gravimetric attractor. The aliens' planet is between us and the suction of the black hole at the center of the galaxy, so it'll work for them. But for you there will be no return.

"Tell us, American peasant? It's what?"

Hadn't I just told him? What was wrong with him? But no, there was something else wrong. Inside me. Waves crashing back and forth in opposing directions. The drug, some sort of truth serum, swelling above a chillingly foreign lock in my mind. I now saw very clearly what I already knew about my star drive. But another wave, also chillingly foreign, had broken over the truth serum wave, locking my jaw shut. I hadn't said a word.

I had to warn them. "It's," I managed. "It's..."

"Tell us!" shrieked Miguel.

"I can't. I can't say. I'd like to, but I can't." Those words I could get out, though just barely.

Miguel's touch was not tender. He jerked my chin up hard and poured a whole lot more of the drink down my throat, choking me with it.

"No, Miguel," I heard Sancho say. "She's had enough."

If I'd thought I was drugged before...

One minute Sancho and Miguel were arguing; then they were gone. I heard nothing. I saw nothing. Then, ever so slowly, I saw an image coming into focus. It was from the original vid of the Wizard of Oz, the scene where Dorothy's dog Toto pulls back the curtain in the chamber of the Great Oz.

Except not only was the little man behind the curtain my Grandpa O, so was the great face of the wizard. "Remember everything," roared the wizard. "And to thine own self be true."

"But there's something wrong with me, Great Oz," I said. "There are things inside me that are not me. If you or that corp I researched for Trix could just help me find a reputable therapy that would—"

"Only you can help yourself," roared the wizard.

Someone was shaking me. The wizard was gone.

"The star drive." It was Sancho's voice this time, soft. "You must tell us."

I could feel that my jaw was still locked; I'd said nothing aloud all that time. I wanted to reach up to touch Sancho's face again. I was so grateful for his tenderness.

"I must tell you," I managed aloud. "You. Your families. You do deserve to know." I paused, horrified by a new thought. "Jupiter's failed star. My very best friend in the whole solar system, Trix, is going with you. The star drive—"

The words "won't work" died in my throat. The toe-move feeling, worse than ever, doubled me over. What in the solar system had I thought I had to tell them about the star drive? But then I remembered. "The star drive will work perfectly for you. I lied when I told you there was a problem, so you'd agree to see me. I wanted to see you because I thought you could help me explain how I got this inaccurate British accent, but it's clearly as much of a mystery to you as it is to me."

Perfect. I'd finally gotten it out. I'd told them what they deserved to know: the truth.

"Perfect score," said Miguel, scrutinizing what I took to be a lie detector. "According to this machine it's 100% certain that she's telling the truth. And I couldn't pour any more truth serum down her throat without killing her." He started removing the straps.

At peace, I vaguely noticed Sancho researching something on a screen before I let the drug close my eyes.

"And Trix," said Sancho, "is her best

friend and is going with us." He caught me when I started to fall sideways again. "How long will she be like this?"

"Half hour. Go. I'll send a maid in to—"

"No, I'll stay with her."

Miguel laughed a bit at that. I heard boots clatter across the floor and huge, metal hinges creak as a door opened and closed. We were alone.

My eyes fluttered open as Sancho kneeled next to me, his face close to mine, holding my hands. "You couldn't have understood what I was thinking in Spanish. You saw her, didn't you."

"Yes. But she was dead."

"If you would close your eyes once more..."

That was easily done. I felt warmth, his breath on my face. Then I felt him gently press his forehead against mine. The drug was starting to wear off but I still felt drowsy, and felt the toe-move feeling again.

The images came slowly at first:

The same magnificent woman, but her big, beautiful dark eyes were open as she danced with her hands high over her head. Her eyes flashed and, like my Grandpa O, she had a wide, utterly infectious, and constant grin.

Next she was kneeling, scooping a litter of playful puppies into her long skirts, and I could hear her laugh, musical as water trickling over rocks.

Then the images started racing, always the grin, always the laugh, and I could feel Sancho's yearning for her racing along with them. Just when I thought I couldn't bear the pain of that yearning any more, the images finally stopped and he spoke.

"No one who remembers my grandmother is still alive except me...and now you."

My eyes were fully open. "Cryopreserved?"

"Yes."

"Then...someday."

"Yes." He gulped back his feelings. "Someday."

"She'll grin again, and laugh that musical laugh."

He touched my face and I could see a hint of her grin in his broad smile. "You could hear it, too?"

"Yes."

And then he kissed my lips. I think it was meant to be quick, perfunctory, at first, but his breath caught and it became longer, hungrier.

I remembered his legs.

My eyes were open but I must still have been drugged to have done what I did next, which was to explore just above his legs.

Actual phys sex. I'd never done it. The first thing that struck me about it was how clumsy and awkward it was. Even a third-rate porn site could have gotten us through the initial stumbling around to get each other's clothes off better. And then there was the question of where to do the deed, never an issue on a porn site where commodious couches materialized out of nowhere. Though I had to admit that Sancho's sweeping all the gadgetry off the table with a single motion, followed by the ease with which he laid me out on top of it, was a grand gesture. And when he first plunged inside me it was a beautiful thing indeed.

But the table was hard beneath me, when he really got down to business, and— magnificent as Sancho was in every phys respect—the man had no technique whatsoever.

And it was over too fast.

Thanks to then-pioneering-and-klutzy faux phys, I was no virgin. I had been gored mightily my first time by the worse-than-third-rate porn site that was all I could afford as a hormone-crazed adolescent, my blood staining an antique rug. But even that porn site had a better idea of how to please a woman than Sancho did.

Frustrated as hell I exploded with, "I wouldn't have paid ten yen for that."

Too late I saw what had been an exquisitely tender look in Sancho's eyes replaced first by surprise, then abject humiliation, then fury. "You're obviously fully conscious now," he said in a dangerously quiet voice. "You can go." With that he leapt off the table, turned on his heel...revealing a great butt in addition to those magnificent legs...and marched out of the room naked.

I scratched my head, then panicked and checked my germ sensors. Yes, they were operational. No, no AIDS 7. I scrambled into my clothes, somewhat mystified by all the moisture down below, and followed Sancho out but he was gone. I headed out of the building, the most wonderful thought in the whole wide solar system being the sight of that ratty old mag car. Besides, I couldn't wait to get home to a good porn site.

SUE HOLLISTER BARR

PART 3

SUE HOLLISTER BARR

A week later Trix' call interrupted me.

Finally signing off on the star drive, I wouldn't have taken a call from anyone else.

"So how's your love life, bot brain?" I greeted her cheerily, my eyes still on the screen where I was just finishing up.

I heard a sniff. That got my attention. I turned to her full body projection standing in...what looked like nothing but a bed sheet. Rather than looking at me she was staring at her toes. Her hair was a worse mess than mine.

"Mart has disappeared." Her natural, rhythmic robo cadence was comforting after all her prior personality work changes, but her voice cracked.

"I found a great new porn site a week ago, called..." When Trix looked up, her eyes stopped me. I knew what I had to do. "Want me to come over and hold you phys?" I wished she was into women sexually, since I'd certainly force myself to be into them too on her behalf, but neither of us were.

Trix was starting to hyperventilate. "No. I cannot be here. Every time I look up I see the wall he leaned against that time he stood naked in the sunlight. Or the chair he always sat in, fidgeting with his magenta muttonchops. Or the bed... I have been sleeping on the floor."

I never thought of that aspect of a real relationship. So that's what people used to go through. Certainly explained a lot of antique vid.

"Nan, I know how you feel about anyone, even me, in your home but I cannot meet you in public; I am...upset, and—"

"Tell the mag car my name of course, then Krusenstern, Alaska."

"Are you sure, Nan?"

"Immediately."

"But you always told me—"

"Never mind anything I told you before."

"Should I bring any—"

"No. Just yourself."

"Do you mind if I am..." Trix tried to run a hand through her hair but a huge snarl stopped her. She seemed to notice the sheet she was wearing for the first time.

"You're fine just as you are."

She started to reach for her ear, forgetting to say goodbye.

"My name, then Krusenstern, Alaska."

She managed another pathetic, voice-cracking, "I have got it," before her projection dissolved.

I sprang into action, sweeping clothes off my sim-wood floor and tossing, I counted, six empty Coca Cola beef stew containers, strewn all over the place, into my sim's recycler. That I could still get that stuff down after last week's fiasco in the Grand Canyon was a testament to my obsession with completing the star drive. I shook my head, realizing I'd again managed to put aside and even forget my personal problems to get that damn star drive done.

Next I fussed with my masterpiece, the elephant it had taken me a year to carve from sim wood, to be sure it was positioned just right, then checked the timepiece in its ear, thinking about the distance Trix had to cover. Flowers, I thought to myself. She'd like flowers in the house, in case she was too depressed to go outside.

I stepped up to the wall and waited for it to make a hole for me. Stepping into my garden, I looked for the latest alien the garden maintenance corp had sent. It had the tool I'd need to dig enough of the flowers up so I wouldn't disturb too much root structure when bringing them into the house temporarily.

I was about to snatch the Don't-Cut-Flowers from the pile of tools when I remembered the completed star drive and paused to look at the alien.

Its blue skin, rippling rhythmically below the armpits, looked even bluer as it stood against the sky, reaching high over its head to prune a climbing rose that snaked up the side of a young Sitka spruce. Against the sky I could just make out a quivering haze that surrounded it. Its source, I assumed, was the frenzied exhalations of vile gases. I remembered them all too well from the alien that died inside my house.

It didn't know it would soon be going

home. None of them did. Reg, Trix, myself, and the typically mysterious corp boss who never called me, were all sworn to secrecy about the alien part of the voyage. The idea was to round them all up at the last minute so they'd have no time to object to leaving their hordes of dying comrades behind. But I wondered if once the Green Party was appeased by their departure, the ones left behind would mysteriously die a whole lot faster...

I'd thought I was doing the best I could for them, and for our overtaxed welfare system. Why would they want to stay on a planet that was slowly killing them? Only now it occurred to me that we'd never been able to get out of them why they left their planet in the first place. I was caught up short, watching the strange creature pruning my roses. Did it want to go home?

It, as was typical of almost all of them, ignored me while I stared at it, its huge slanting eyes never looking away from the roses, its long fingers a blur as they deftly deadheaded the spent blooms.

I picked up the Don't-Cut-Flowers, and started to walk away but found myself turning to look at it again. In profile I noticed for the first time that its beaklike mouth was a bit like the snowy's.

"I'm taking the Don't-Cut-Flowers," I told it, which wasn't at all necessary.

It looked at me, apparently feeling my talking to it demanded that much, then went back to its pruning.

"I wonder... Do you miss your home planet?"

Was it my imagination or did it look at me warily? Perhaps it knew that people didn't usually engage in idle conversation with aliens.

"I know. You can't really speak. I'm just curious... Do you know what direction your home planet is from here?"

Silence. Then the rustling of the vegetation as it extracted one hand from its work and pointed in what I already knew was the right direction.

"Huh." I scratched my head and did my best to look dumb, not hard since I felt dumb. "Our planet is beautiful. Would you still like to go home to yours?"

I knew it could shake its head yes and no. But instead it stared at me for a good long time, huge eyes getting even bigger. Finally it shook its head yes.

"Huh," is what I said before shrugging casually and heading back to the flowers nearer the house. But once my back was turned to it I allowed myself to smile. I didn't know what I would have done if it had shaken its head no.

I brought in flowers I thought Trix would like, then checked in the ear of my elephant. Few minutes left so I brought up my screen. With a last look in the direction of the alien pruning my roses, I finished my final sign off on the star drive and hit send.

I was done. Out of work...since one of the many things I'd neglected lately was lining up my next contract...but done.

A little time left, and I couldn't think of anything else to do to prepare for Trix. I got something cold to drink from my sim. I ran idle fingers over my masterpiece, the elephant. Then I indulged an utterly random whim.

First I made sure anything like that cold drink that I might want to find in the dark was within reach. Then I frowned, trying to remember the name, pulled my earlobe, and said, "Sancho Diego Jose Francisco de Panza Juan Cipriano de la Castilla." The house went dead and dark. I sipped my drink while waiting through the recording about this being the secure line of someone who only communicated in dead rooms, phys. When prompted I stated my name and was trying to figure out what I was going to state for my business. But I wasn't asked. Instead I was immediately told to come to the same destination, whenever I wished. Call disconnected. House went live. That was easy.

Considering my last words to Sancho, I surmised they would either shoot me on sight, or did in fact have what my Grandpa O would have called character.

The sound of a large object settling amidst the vegetation around my house announced Trix' mag car. My house made a hole for me to exit next to that sound before Trix got out.

But she'd gotten no further than opening the mag car's door.

I found her curled up in the fetal position, clinging to small things I couldn't see. Trinkets left by Mart? Gently I smoothed the hair back from her face. "So, how many nanobots does it take to..." I trailed off. Trix had started to smile weakly, but probably only for my sake. "What have you got there?"

She stopped clinging, releasing her grip enough for me to see the two objects she held: an old pipe and a small red ball. I was taken aback; I'd forgotten. Years ago she'd asked me to hit undo after I'd tossed these objects into my sim's recycler and bring them to her instead.

"If it is not too much trouble, could you tell me more stories of your Grandpa O?"

Grandpa O. Her vicarious haven, too? All she could think of to cling to and she'd never even met the man. Or even seen another human being until she hit adolescence. "Of course, Trix. Let's just get you into the house first."

I got her inside and tossed the sheet,

which frankly stank, into my sim's recycler. I then ran a tub full of hot water with the soothing, antidepressant scents of sandalwood and lavender thrown in. I eased her in amidst the bubbles, lay her head back on a waterproof pillow, and got to work slowly unknotting her hair while stroking her head.

"So, one time when I was very young Grandpa O—"

"I loved him."

"My Grandpa O?"

"Yes. But I was talking about Mart. But I do not even want to think about Mart. Go on about Grandpa O."

"Grandpa O had resolved to teach me how to be self-reliant, no matter what happened, so he wrapped some cloth around my head so I couldn't see."

"He would have wanted me to be self-reliant, too."

"My Grandpa O?"

"No, Mart. We were headed in that direction. He was so nice to me, so supportive."

"I thought you didn't want to—"

"I do not. I definitely do not. Go on about your Grandpa O."

"So at first I stumbled into things but—"

"If only I had not been...upset about the things I have learned about the aliens while preparing to accompany them home. Maybe Mart was...upset because he got me the contract."

"I thought I suggested you try my corp."

"Mart broke his constant promise to always stay in touch, no matter what. One minute he was all tickles and smiles and the next..." Trix convulsed in tears.

I reached into the water and wrapped my arms around her. After a while I poured more essential oils into the tub and tried to rub the tension out of her back and neck. Then, with the knots mostly gone, I started to wash her hair, taking plenty of time to rub her scalp and massage her temples. She calmed a bit.

"So, another time my Grandpa O wanted to be sure I could always find my way home. He used his sleeve to wipe the dust off the phys controls for an archaic helicopter-like thing he'd built and tossed me inside. I'd never seen him use it before and didn't even know it worked. It looked ridiculous, especially because it was made of odd pieces of scrap metal he'd scavenged. One cockeyed piece even said 'Stromboli Bakery, best cannolis anywhere' sideways.

"I didn't know what a cannoli was then, but I was pretty sure it didn't have anything to do with aviation. Damn thing didn't even work off magnetism, but rather a loud engine of some sort that he actually poured some lethal-smelling fuel into. Knowing my Grandpa O I figured the whole thing, and most especially the fuel he poured from a container he'd carefully labeled 'olive oil,' was totally illegal."

Trix actually smiled at that last, then made a faux pouty face and said, "Grandpa O would not have given me a hard time about my illegal personality work!"

I boxed her ears playfully.

"Stop! My head hurts enough whenever I see you."

I splashed water in her face while she protested amidst a giggle or two, and went on.

"But the damn thing actually flew, and I don't mean hovered above the ground like a mag car, I mean went up and up and up and up. I couldn't believe it at first, and it apparently couldn't either because the engine sputtered and stopped. In the silence that followed I could hear the wind whistling through all the odd pieces of metal sticking out all over the place as we fell back down towards the ground like a stone.

"First my Grandpa O stopped grinning, and even let the soggy cigar stub in the corner of his mouth drop to the contraption's floor. That's how I knew the situation was serious. Next he grabbed my wrist hard with his right hand. Of course anyone not knowing my Grandpa O would have thought grabbing my wrist wouldn't help but—"

"Your Grandpa O would have flown himself, just by flapping his left hand, if that is what it would have taken to save you."

This time I kissed the top of her soapy head. "You got it, Trix. But instead he used his left hand to perfectly execute a move he'd forced me to practice for years."

Trix looked puzzled. "What was that?"

"The exact same move that Duke Morrison knocked Razor Ruddock out with in 1995: a deadly left hook to the engine."

Trix smirked. "I should have seen that coming."

"Apparently the engine didn't either. It sputtered back to life immediately and we flew back up. That engine didn't misbehave again."

I'd finished washing Trix' hair and was massaging her shoulders when I felt a jerk of returning tension in her muscles and saw a look of agony break over her face. I assumed she was thinking of Mart but what she said was, "Then what happened?"

I hurried on. "Grandpa O took us deep into the vast wilderness that surrounded his ramshackle house. All the while he was going on about something called an Australian walkabout, and everything he'd ever taught me about how to survive in the wild and find my way home. For most of the trip he had me blindfolded so I couldn't see where he was taking me."

Trix started to relax again. "Then what happened?"

I was the one starting to get tense this time, as I remembered. "He fucking dropped me in the middle of the goddamn wilderness and left me there. Just before leaving...but after taking a pull of whiskey to fortify himself without offering <u>me</u> any...he leaned in close to hiss in a whisper, 'Remember everything. Everything I ever taught you, everything you ever knew or even will know in this or any other lifetime. And to thine own self be true.'

"He left me with nothing but myself...no food, no compass, no blanket to keep warm, not even a knife. Terrified, I watched him fly away until all that was left of him was a tiny speck in the sky. Then I strained to hear that ridiculous engine until I had to accept that all I was hearing was the cold, merciless wind."

The tub water sloshed furiously as Trix lifted an arm free so she could reach up and squeeze my hand.

"Alone in so vast a wilderness, I tried to replace my Grandpa of Oz with something else at least somewhat outside of myself.

Frantic, I spent hours repeating the survival skills I'd been taught, over and over, as if through repetition I could give them a separate physical presence. Then I noticed I'd been eating berries without even thinking about it, carefully avoiding the poisonous ones, and I hadn't even gotten to the food part of my survival skills.

"I looked at my hand, frozen in the act of picking a good berry that was surrounded by poisonous ones because the two vines were intertwined. These in turn were intertwined with a young tree. As I watched, an ant carefully picked its way through all this interconnected stuff and started out across the back of my hand, tickling me with its footsteps.

"All my thoughts, even the Universal English language itself, were sucked out of me as if by a vacuum. I know this sounds silly, but first I was the ant, then I was the poisonous berry it had by then crawled onto, then I was the nutrients its roots were extracting from the soil. Finally I was everything, as all the dividers that separate one thing from another dissolved.

"Determination. After a long while I came back to myself, but it was a new, far stronger sense of self. It was as if becoming everything else had been like striking the tuning fork needed to truly find me."

Trix dropped my hand. "What?"

"Suffice it to say that when my Grandpa O said he wanted to be sure I could always find my way home, he wasn't just talking about my phys way back to his house. He was talking about the home that's inside of me."

"How did you find your way back to his house?"

"By the sun and the stars and noting which side of a tree had moss on it. Wasn't easy. Had to sleep in nests of leaves I made in ravines. Got really sick of those berries. Wasn't until years later that I learned Grandpa O had only gone as far back as he had to so I couldn't hear when he landed, then backtracked on foot. He was never more than twenty meters from my side."

"Dear Grandpa O."

"Yeah. Till he went to Mars."

"Were you mad at him for that?"

"No. I can't be mad at Grandpa O."

Trix was looking up at me. "You look mad. You look like you used to look all the time when you had your anger problem, but you do not seem to have your anger problem anymore."

"I was never really mad at Grandpa O, I was mad at...other things."

"You were mad at everything."

"But not Grandpa O."

"Because?"

"Because no one could be mad at Grandpa O."

"But there were only the two of you, so who else could you be mad at?"

It felt like a psychological blowtorch had been turned my way, but I pushed that agony aside and then remembered all the other stuff I'd been pushing aside. I wanted to concentrate on Trix, but I did have one quick question, since I could no longer be sure I could even hear it anymore. "Am I still speaking with some kind of British accent?"

Trix answered yes without a moment's hesitation.

I got her out of the tub, printed her some clothes and even got her to agree to eat some Coca Cola beef stew in the garden. But every now and then she'd flinch, as if in sudden physical pain, and I knew thoughts of Mart had ambushed her. So I did my best to keep it lively, hoping to ambush her myself with so many different things to think about that she would have as little time to think of Mart as possible. I heard the alien working near the table where we ate and, in my role as court jester, I even tried to distract Trix by suggesting it join us for some beef stew. I thought I was being funny, though I felt a little guilty about doing it at the poor alien's expense. But Trix suddenly flinched so hard she all but doubled over.

"What did I say wrong?"

"That is when Mart left me."

"When?"

Trix looked sharply in the direction of the alien; I couldn't hear it working anymore and turned to see it staring back at Trix, its huge eyes getting even bigger. Finally Trix got up, started to sob again, and ran for the house.

I followed her in and found her curled up in the fetal position in my papasan chair. I guessed the time for trying to let her build up some strength in normalcy, by distracting her with other things, was over.

"When did Mart leave you?"

"When I told him the aliens cannot eat anything unless what they eat is alive."

"You don't mean...while they're eating it?"

"Yes."

I no longer felt the least bit of guilt over anything I could ever say at the expense of an alien. "Trix, that's ridiculous; how do you know that?"

"Remember the job Mart got me is to escort them back to their home planet as soon as you complete the star drive?"

"The job Mart got you? What's he got to do with our current corp? Anyway, yes, I know that's your job..." What I'd been wondering, since I had just completed the star drive, was if she'd be in any shape to go.

"Because of that the welfare people have

given me more freedom to observe the aliens over long periods of time than anyone. They do not eat often, which is why no one ever sees them doing it, and they do not eat much, but when they do eat, they think anything that is already dead is disgusting."

SUE HOLLISTER BARR

PART 4

SUE HOLLISTER BARR

ne week.

One hundred Grandpa O stories. Trix was finally improved enough that I could begin to think of myself again.

I lied to that corp that helped people with personality work damage, "proving" I'd had genetic work done by claiming the effects were constant. In truth I'd only gotten through the whole phone call as Lydia Bennet by dragging and dropping a copy of *Pride and Prejudice* onto the bot interviewer's eyes. But it wasn't visible to the bot, who told me I qualified for a phys attend with them.

I found Trix curled up in my papasan chair, smiling softly as dawn bathed her face through the walls I'd cleared so she could see outside. Not wanting to break the spell, I explained everything quickly and told her I should be back in time to watch the sun set over the water behind her.

But she grabbed my hand. "Only because Mart knew where to take me..." She trailed off sadly, but then recovered. "I am the

successfully restored survivor of enough
genetics to change an amoeba into an
elephant! You do not want me to go along
with you? Watch your back?"

She had a point, but I tried not to let my
face show it. I wasn't sure what I was in for
but didn't think it would include the
tranquility I felt Trix still needed.

"No, bot brain, you relax and eat more
Coca Cola beef stew. You might want to take
a stroll outside in the late afternoon, when the
sun slants low and sparkles through the
tundra. All I ask you to solemnly swear is that
you'll stay away from the snowies' precious
rats."

Several tubes later the mag car came up
on a town I hadn't seen in a very long time.

As I soared down into the city proper,
someone on a track above me littered, tossing
something that sparkled in the sunlight. It
cascaded in a long, spiral descent past
shimmering buildings whose current, shared
theme was Impressionist painting. One
graceful, asymmetrical tower was wrapped in
everything Monet ever painted at Giverny.

Delicately animated, its sheaves of wheat blew in the wind and, taking poetic license, plump children ran across the arched bridges. Maybe Grandpa O had been wrong to teach me to hate holo décor. Especially since the cloyingly gauche Rococo had at last lost its perma-hold. But that feeling vanished when the mag car reached the destination the corp had given me.

"What the fuck?"

The car printed some scrap of paper for me before opening the door.

I snatched the piece of paper, dully noting some fine print about the clandestine nature of their business precluding their giving a mag car the exact address, and stepped out onto a public walkway.

Ads tornadoed around me. I tried to read the corp's meter marking address off the piece of paper. But the holo of a truly seductive man lifted my chin with more faux phys force than even my true phys body could overcome. He was presenting me with a rose, accompanied by painfully bad poetry and a plea to seize the "opportunity" to invest in a newly discovered asteroid's gold mine.

I feigned a bashful blush as I accepted the rose with one hand. Then I seized the "opportunity" and demurely looked away...at my other hand holding the piece of paper with the address: 47.88/21.45/98.30.

I thought meter markings were supposed to be at eye level but could find none, straining to see past all the holography. For no particular reason, perhaps to rest my eyes from the ads' frantic flurry, I started to look down at my own feet.

Simultaneously another gorgeous holo man, a giant animated mockingbird selling sims, and a panda selling pre-fab housing, all used faux phys to lift my chin.

"Methinks thou doth protest too much." I couldn't phys fight them but they couldn't control my eyes. I looked straight down and saw the meter markings, subtly visible on the walkway just in front of my toes: 52.34/27.22/98.30.

Okay, at least I was at the right altitude, high above the city's floor, almost visible in its dark obscurity through all the transparent walkways.

I took a big step forward: 53.21/28.13/98.30. Nope, wrong direction. I did a 180 and slowly made my way to the correct address with my ad entourage, now all holo men in various states of undress and arousal. I could tell when I reached my destination without looking down because the ads collectively threw up their hands. Then they all morphed into various products designed to increase the sexual libido they'd unanimously concluded I needed. I gathered that other people, who were heading where I was, had been dropped in the middle of that walkway before. When all the libido-enhancing products gathered to conceal one location, the size of a doorway, I drew the correct conclusion and walked through it.

A woman stood in front of me in a lab coat, her hair and face refreshingly natural after the glitz of the ads. But she had her hands on her hips, looking annoyed.

"You call yourself a fellow scientist yet you take weeks to find us and show up looking for a cure?"

"Huh?"

"I could have been fucking cryopreserved without finding out what happened to my first human experiment."

Even though she was staring straight at me I looked around to see if there was anyone else in the all-white room. I'd never laid eyes on her before. Was she out of her mind?

She spoke slowly, as if to a child. "What. Took. You. So. Long?"

"I... I really don't understand why, but I was more obsessed with getting a particular assignment completed for work than I've ever been. I think toes could have fallen off and I wouldn't have attended to it."

She looked like the proverbial light bulb had gone off. "Of course. I forgot about that component."

"Huh?"

"Never mind. Have a seat."

I started to sit in a white chair, the only place to sit in the room, but something stopped me.

That astounded the woman. "Do you remember..." She paused, then went on. "Do you have a feeling of déjà vu, as if you've been here before?"

"No." Nuts, totally nuts. I was beginning to tune her out and wonder where else I could get help. Sachs again?

She relaxed. "Well then, have a seat."

"If you don't mind I'll stand."

That earned me a sharp, wary look.

Great. Just what I needed: a paranoid mad scientist.

"So start at the beginning and tell all. And know this: I can't help you unless you're completely honest. What's the first you remember of your supposedly 'uninterrupted'..." She paused to rake me with a contemptuous look since I'd dropped the Lydia Bennet act. "...personality change?"

I had no idea why the woman was willing to waive the uninterrupted requirement. But my rising anxiety over sitting in the white chair was at least equally illogical. So I told her all, surprised that she didn't react with any interest. However...just when I thought I'd put her to sleep by stating the ridiculously obvious, that my British accent was ridiculously inaccurate...she perked right up and got annoyed again.

"What do you mean inaccurate?"

"I'm pronouncing 'r's,'" I answered, dumbfounded by the question.

Her eyes went wide. "Oh." She called up a screen I couldn't see and made a note, then shrugged. "Who knew?"

"What?"

"Never mind. I keep forgetting you'll remember this conversation." She glanced at the empty chair behind me. "Unless... Are you sure you wouldn't like to sit down?"

"No, thanks." What was wrong with the woman? I'd never had a memory problem. I went on, but was wondering if I could ask the psycho if someone else was available to help me without annoying her further.

She looked sleepy again and took no further notes until I got to the part about "hearing" what the snowy flying over my house was feeling. That got her taking notes at a furious pace and grilling me with questions. Typical healthcare professional. She'd probably start snoring if I told her I had

AIDS 7, yet she woke up for the one part I didn't mind. However, I did lie some about the incident with Sancho, making him a phys date, and replacing the truth serum with drinking so much alcohol that I eventually passed out.

The woman was frowning. "You only experience telepathy when not fully conscious, as if you'd been put to..." She trailed off; another light bulb seemed to have gone off for her. "Same state of consciousness as when you were first given..." She trailed off again, furiously taking notes.

"You mean because this was somehow done remotely, while I slept?"

She gave me a funny look before answering, "Yeah, right. Continue your story."

I did. To try to refocus the flake on what I wanted help with, I said I liked the telepathy. I needed help with the blocks in my mind, things I couldn't get to or at least couldn't say aloud or even remember when I needed to. I could also do without Lydia Bennet and the bad British accent.

"Only one person liked it," I added, though it was unimportant, possibly my mind rebelling against the struggle to convey what was important to an annoyed nut. And then it came to me, the person I'd been trying to remember in the Grand Canyon, when it might have been important. "Trix' boyfriend, Mart." I said aloud. "God, I hate magenta eyes."

"Your friend Trix'...boyfriend?"

"Yeah, the bastard. They were living together until a week ago. Then he disappeared." I didn't think Trix would care if I told a stranger, and got a little of the anger I'd avoided dwelling on in Trix' presence off my chest. But I had to stop this and get us back on track.

"They were living together...a week ago?"

Oh Jupiter's failed star. Like the telepathy she was again fixating on the wrong things. And she looked worse than annoyed now; she looked angry. I tried to refocus her by asking, "Can you help me?"

Now she was pacing and appeared to be fighting back tears. Nuts. So far out there she was in intergalactic orbit. No wonder I let almost everything she said go in one ear and out the other. Getting useful information from her was as likely as getting any from That Stupid Underling From Work.

Wildly overwrought, she almost sank into the chair but caught herself abruptly and stood beside it, glaring at me. I couldn't say I was comforted that we shared the same irrational aversion to the chair.

"Help you? Like I—like your friend Trix got help?" She started pacing again.

"Yes. Her boyfriend got her completely back to normal—through someone, somewhere—except there's just a teeny bit she can't remember, and her head still hurts sometimes."

She paused her pacing and stared at me, smirking. "You might want to stay away from your 'friend' Trix when that happens."

"How can you help me?"

"With Trix? I can't, but I will tell you it'll only happen once, few minutes' duration."

"Huh?" I doubted the idiot knew Trix or had any idea what she was saying. I was praying she'd refer me to someone else. "I meant me."

"You?" She shrugged. "I can't."

Great. Now we were getting somewhere. "Who can?"

"No one."

"You must have someone else working here. A second opinion?"

"I'm the only one here."

Shit. I could feel my shoulders sagging until they threatened to hit the floor. I should have paid more attention to the woman. "There's nowhere else I can go? And there's nothing, nothing in the whole wide solar system, you can do to help me?"

She shook her head no.

I stared deep into her eyes. I wondered what it was going to be like to spend the rest of my life like this. I wondered just who I'd thought I was to deem her the nutty one. "Is that because it's intermittent?"

"Partially. Intermittent means sometimes you're Lydia Bennet but sometimes you're Nan. That's why our ads insist on uninterrupted. As it is, if I take out Lydia

Bennet, I'll take you right out with it."

"But there must be something..." Sachs again? No, they never helped, either. Maybe it was just part of the human condition to be imperfect.

"You don't like Trix' 'boyfriend' do you?"

What did that have to do with... "No, but maybe we're all flawed."

"Mart is more than flawed!"

How did she know?

"Let's just say he doesn't keep promises," she all but spat through her teeth.

That was true. Poor Trix.

"So no one should feel obligated to keep any promises made to him." The woman seemed focused now. Furious, but focused. She came up close, staring into my eyes. "Listen carefully: There's something in you."

"Yeah, that's why—"

"Listen and don't interrupt. Something useful. There are no documented cases of anyone's natural personality being dominant enough to overcome authenticated genetic personality work to the extent you have."

"How do we know it was genetic? I never

left home. I never agreed to—"

"Will you shut the fuck up! Just trust that I know. The blocks in your mind? I can fix that. But Lydia Bennet and the British accent? Only you can overcome those, if it's possible."

With that she did a quick 180 and left me alone. Returning with an injection, she grabbed my upper arm, but I wheeled away. "Wait, before you do anything I want to know—" But she had already stabbed me with it, hitting the funny bone in my elbow where she injected me instead. It hurt like hell.

Then she choked back a violent sob and shoved me out the doorway.

My elbow was killing me; the ads re-attacked. Trying to walk back through the doorway, I just hit what must have been the phys door she locked behind me.

I heard a buzz in my ear.

That Stupid Underling From Work.

Okay. Okay. I reprogrammed my phone to call him Reg before answering, despite heroic efforts to intervene by a naked holo man selling sexual-libido-enhancing drugs.

Reg's copper eyes were squinting at a screen that I, too, could see. "This is a secure line, Nan, and we've got a problem with a weight overage. And I've got to sign off on the ship by the end of the day, or we won't make next week's launch date."

Trix had to be ready to go next week? I'd have to go with her; she wouldn't be able to manage alone yet. Especially with dangerous aliens. But just as that started to worry me I got a completely different toe-move feeling. Something brand new. "Do you know that my phone—obviously inadvertently reprogrammed one time when I must have muttered my true feelings about you—was referring to you as 'That Stupid Underling From Work'?"

What the fuck? How did that get out of my mouth?

"What was that, Nan?"

Thank Jupiter's failed star! I started to say "nothing" but what started to come out instead was an exact repeat of what I said before. What saved me was the naked holo man, who faux physed clapping both hands over my mouth, winked, and then shoved the drugs he was selling in front me. Unable to speak—thankfully, since I gathered I'd at least initially swung to an extreme where there were no blocks remaining on what I might say—I watched Reg's screen as he scrolled furiously. Some secure call, assuming there was any such thing to begin with: he hadn't remembered to make his screen invisible to others.

"Nan, why did you add a weight allowance for 'food supplies for the aliens'?"

I got rid of the naked holo man by clicking a request for more information on the drugs he was selling. The new toe-move feeling subsided but my elbow was killing me, and I had to get home. "I was trying to cover what you obviously left..."

I was going to add "out" but I noticed an odd thing on Reg's screen: Under food supplies for the humans were all the usual stores you'd expect, but under food supplies for the aliens all I could see was a list of the human passengers with what I assumed were their weights in parentheses.

"But, Nan, we already counted the human passenger weight in the passenger manifest. So what you added is a duplication I can eliminate, right?"

Dully, as if someone else were speaking, I heard myself say, "Right."

"Thanks, Nan. Sorry about your friend Trix, by the way. When the boss told me she was your friend, and he told me not to tell you he'd told me, I never dreamed you'd have enough business acumen to know our little secret and go ahead with it. But I did finally follow your good example and see sense, when the boss offered me a really sweet bonus. Anyway, gotta go. Bye."

"What?" But one of the old toe-move feelings interrupted and I realized I was glad I bought my bonnet, if it was only for the fun of having another band-box. No! Trix? Eaten alive?

A screech, followed by a roar, reverberated through every cell in my body. My Grandpa O, as the Wizard of Oz, and the nutty woman I'd just seen, as the Wicked Witch of the West, spoke as one within me:

"Only you can overcome this."

Determination. All my thoughts, even the Universal English language itself, were sucked out of me as if by a vacuum. I felt the city, then I was the city. Then, as if a giant tuning fork had been struck, I came crashing back to myself. I had to call Trix first, to find out what she knew before calling Reg back, but— for starters—forever fuck all things Lydia Bennet.

I ordered a mag car, noting with pleasure how fast they were to rescue someone from a public walkway, clicked "no" multiple times to the naked holo man's drug offer, and got in.

As soon as I pulled the safety mesh over me I double-pulled my ear. "Secure line: Trix."

Nothing.

I tried again.

Nothing.

Could she have drifted off to sleep?

At least there was a week before launch, with no blocks in my mind to stop me from stopping Trix.

The mag car was carrying me up toward

the first tube heading home. Except for the space elevator in what was once Central Park, Manhattan glittered beneath me, its buildings having changed theme since I arrived. The Impressionist painters had been replaced by the Realists. Edward Hopper's 20th century painting of *Early Sunday Morning* spiraled around the two tallest towers I could still see, sporting 19th century row houses the city had since lost. Their awnings snapped in a non-existent breeze, lit by Hopper's impossibly serene, profoundly silent light.

Either way, a long twilight of the Rococo, delicious in its excesses but decadent, had been cleansed by the Enlightenment and what followed. I could only hope Reg would eventually catch up and recycle his brocade vest.

Once in the tube I double pulled my ear again. "Secure line: Trix." Again, nothing. And then it hit me: Not even the option to leave a message?

Tube ads flashed past me, their particular rhythm hypnotic as always. But I couldn't get home fast enough.

As promised I was home in time for sunset over the water, but my house didn't look right. It took me a minute to peg it: no light. The garden didn't even light up around me when the mag car settled in among the roses.

I got out, stumbling over some shrubbery while I still had some light from my departing mag car. I stood next to a wall, waiting for it to let me in.

Nothing.

Perhaps stupidly, I stumbled through a few more rose bushes, cursing, and tried another part of my house.

Still nothing.

Then I saw it, only because the sunset sparkling over the water backlit it: another mag car.

The house's one permanent, emergency door opened and Trix ran out holding, of all things, a lit candle. "You will never, never, never guess who is here!"

"You're okay?"

It was a stupid question. Trix' face, ablaze in the sunset, was wreathed in smiles. She was literally jumping for joy, too busy giggling to answer.

"Why's the house dead?"

"Oh that. I do not know. Maybe you did not pay your bills?" She laughed at her own joke. "Come in!"

Maybe it was just using the emergency door for the first time ever but a shiver went up my spine as Trix pulled me into my own house, still giggling. I looked back over my shoulder as she closed the door behind me. Was that the alien, still working in the garden, that I saw silhouetted by the sunset along with the strange mag car?

Trix stopped to frown at me, now that my face was illuminated by the sunset visible through the walls I'd left clear for her. "What is wrong with you? Are you mad again? Are you still angry at Grandpa O?"

"Angry at Grandpa O! I told you I could never be..." New toe-move feeling. No blocks in my mind. "No, you're right; I am angry at Grandpa O, for leaving me when he went to Mars." Integration: it was as if I could feel the new and old weird things blend with the rest of me. But a final, pure surge of the new, as if its swan song, hit me hard. Every last block crumbled. "No, I was right in the first place. No one could be mad at Grandpa O. The person I've been mad at all this time was myself for being too damn stupid and stubborn to go with him on the last ship to Mars."

Birdlike, Trix tilted her head to watch me. "Know what?"

"What?" I asked, wiping away bitter tears. The adventure of Mars, a world where there had never been brocade vests. But much, much more than that: the years with Grandpa O, lost forever. Was that why I could never bear to replace him with another, phys man? "What, Trix, what?"

"You are no longer talking with a British accent."

I heard something. A shape emerged from the dark interior of my house. "Shame, my dearest dear," said a male voice. Mart was looking at me, but slid his arm around Trix. "Ah, Syb... But one should never trust a woman scorned."

Trix turned toward him at that. "The woman who you got to fix me? Except this headache I only get when Nan is around?" She winked at me playfully, then turned back to Mart. "This Syb wanted..." Trix frowned, puzzling it out, then started to hyperventilate.

"But I did not want her, Best Beloved," Mart said, embracing Trix warmly.

Trix sniffled. Then her smile twitched into its fullest glory, her eyes wide and childlike. "Thank you for wanting me."

They kissed, on fire in the light of the sunset. I smiled, but took Trix' forgotten candle before she tilted the wax onto my floor. Even with it I was glad I'd left the house transparent for Trix; without the full scope of the sunset we couldn't have seen much.

They started ripping clothes off. I guessed my questions about Reg could wait that long. I went back outside through the emergency door.

No alien was visible. As late as sunset? I must have been mistaken before. Hearing moans from the house, I walked out beyond the garden, into the tundra.

Breathing the night air deeply was as refreshingly clean as drinking cold water until... I was also breathing in something vile, but vaguely familiar, and I heard the tundra rustle in front of me, upwind.

A twig snapped behind me. I wheeled.

"You are among friends, my dearest dear." Sunset fired Mart's face.

"That was..."

He grinned. "Quick? She's asleep now. Must have needed it."

"Alas, too true," I said, borrowing the flowery speech he'd just dropped. Then I looked at him sharply. "Are you back to stay?"

I didn't understand the look he gave me. Or the cruel laugh that followed. "Shame you didn't keep the accent. Then, maybe, I could have trusted others to do my dirty work."

The accent. Yes, I remembered he'd liked it but— Duh, the woman who gave me the shot in the elbow: She did know Trix and Mart.

All I saw was the slightest flicker in the

sunset reflected off of Mart. All I knew was that one minute I was standing, looking at him. The next minute I was airborne, looking in the exact opposite direction, blinded by the sunset and sucking in that faint, odious smell. I landed hard on my back, just barely turning my head back around to avoid its being smashed into the ground. Mart seemed to shake his head no in the direction of the sunset. The tundra I'd displaced swung back over my head to pelt me with twigs, leaves and seeds.

My candle was gone, but sunset flared off what Mart arched high above me: a nasty-looking knife.

I rolled. He compensated easily. The only thing that saved me was that he was just a step too close. I took him down with a scissor kick around his ankles. The knife clattered against a stone inches from my head, then ricocheted to cut my cheek. I grabbed it as I got to my feet, but he was faster, snatching the knife away from me with one hand while he threw another punch with the other.

I saw it coming this time, dodged and dropped. But the tundra held me captive till he grabbed me from behind and yanked me to my feet. I barely managed to knock the knife out of his hand again with my sore elbow.

With both of us on our feet, but him behind me, I could feel him spreading his legs wide. Maybe for stability. But I managed to throw my arms over my head and reach back far enough to clasp the back of his neck. I swung my legs up in front of me, till my knees reached my chin, then used their momentum to swing back hard between his legs while arching my back and yanking his head over mine. I landed on my belly. He somersaulted onto the ground in front of me.

I scrambled to my feet first and ran for the emergency door to my house, desperately trying to remember how to lock it since I never had. But he shoved us both into the house with a flying tackle. Airborne, I came down hard, but managed to fall correctly, distributing the force evenly throughout my body.

I got to my knees just in time to block his

knife thrust with my forearm, my other arm braced against the floor. Spinning on one knee, I kicked his legs out from under him. The knife clattered across the floor, coming to rest in a last remaining puddle of sunset. But he was more stable on my floor than he'd been in the tundra, and my strike wasn't hard enough. He regained his footing. Fortunately I'd used my kicking leg to get to my feet, too. But I didn't get my arms up in time.

His hands landed like a vice grip on my neck. I tried to go for his face but his arms were much longer than mine. Except for a few poorly leveraged karate chops at his locked elbows, my arms were useless.

I didn't realize how quickly I'd feel the effects of that relentless clamp around my neck. Already my kicks were getting rubbery and ineffectual. I did the stupid thing: I clawed pathetically at the hands he'd buried in my neck.

I heard a snore from Trix, realizing with a sharp stab of anguish that I could no longer protect her. Too late, too late. Mart was pushing me back, back, until I hit something behind me. He was leaning into his work, no longer concerned about my wildly flailing arms as he bent his elbows until his face was directly in front of mine, a slow smile spreading over it. He jerked his grip tighter; my vision went black. I felt him jerk again; I no longer knew whether I was still standing. But those were all phys losses; in my isolated blackness I was fully conscious, screaming in anguish. Then there was just the vaguest residual hint of the old toe-move feeling.

Suddenly I was seeing again, but I wasn't at home. I was in a room I'd never seen before, staring across a table at—yes, at myself with paisleys crawling across the wallpaper behind me. I was in my brown business suit, which I hadn't worn since that day…at the beginning of my obsession with the star drive…that I'd slept all day. Telepathy…

I felt something around my neck. Mart was readjusting his hands; strangling me was hard work. In the midst of it, I got my senses back for a moment and stared at him.

Slept all day. Boss was supposed to call.

Woke up in my business suit. Always knew I hated magenta eyes.

My instinct was to claw at his hands but logic, as cold as his smile, took in my location. My fingers jerked behind me as I oozed in and out of consciousness. Finally I found my masterpiece and reached behind it. It was small but I made sure it was pointed upward. Then I swung it around between us and fired the cross-bow up under the solar plexus and into my boss' heart.

He thudded to the floor in a widening puddle of blood. "Frigid bitch!"

Possibly true.

He spasmed, grimaced, looked stupid for a moment, and stuttered through a last breath.

I wiped saliva from my mouth and choked when I tried to swallow.

Was he dead?

I was about to be sure when I heard something behind me and spun around. It was Trix, holding her head in agony.

I explained everything. I could see she struggled mightily with herself, moaning in pain. As I stood over the body of her beloved, I could hardly blame her. But she finally came toward me, her arms stretched out to comfort me. I was about to warn her not to trip on the knife when I noticed it wasn't there anymore. And then I remembered.

To give her credit, she was fast, and I was at a great disadvantage because I didn't want to hurt her, but after a few minutes struggle she suddenly released her fingers and let me take the knife.

"The pain, the pain in my head. It is gone now."

"I know, Trix. Don't worry. It won't come back."

"What was I doing just now? I must have been—"

I explained the warning the woman who'd worked on us both had given me.

"Syb and Mart?" Trix started to cry.

I put my arm around her. "Trix, we have to get out of here, and we have to tell the TexMexes not to board that ship, which can only be done phys."

"But your house is dead."

"Mart must have done that."

"We cannot order a mag car. When your house does go live it will have to report a dead body."

"Two birds; one stone."

I was sorry to force a hysterically heartbroken Trix to help me, but it took both of us to drag Mart's body close enough to his mag car for it to open. I hadn't been sure it would work, or that the car wouldn't report him dead, but gambled successfully that few would commit murder in such a confined space.

To be safe I even used Mart's fingers to punch in "Lexington, TexMex."

"What was that thud in the back?"

"Nothing, Trix, nothing. Just your nerves."

We were off, me on one side, Trix on the other, her lover I'd killed crammed tightly between us. I think I could have stood it if she'd howled, questioned the explanation I'd given her, anything...even a sniffle.

In silence we entered the tube. Something I heard this time thudded in the back by the air compartment.

Trix said nothing.

No blackout this time so I'd killed the interior lights. The three of us were only lit, eerily, by the tube ads flowing over us. Smiley-faced kittens peddling moon resorts swam over Trix' unblinking face of stone. Extreme adventurers selling rock-climbing expeditions in the asteroid belt passed effortlessly over the arrow still protruding from Mart. Something caught my eye, and I looked down to see, ironically, Beautiful Nuskin ads undulating across my blood-stained hands. An eternity later we were spit out into the blackness of night, heading for the Grand Canyon.

When we tumbled into it, I knocked my face into the air gauge, oddly almost empty despite a relatively short trip. Then Mart's body flopped forward, sickeningly, and fell back across Trix as we leveled out at the bottom. Still she didn't move; I wasn't even sure she blinked.

This time I could see the huge stone door to the TexMex bunker open to reveal Sancho waiting, then close behind us. When I heard the mag car door open I braced myself, remembering Miguel's reception last time.

Vile fumes filled the car. The same agile blue fingers that deadheaded my roses so well dug into my face, intent on removing my eyes. Its beak-like mouth went for my neck.

I blocked, but Sancho saved me. With one graceful motion he yanked the alien off me and sliced off its head with the sword I'd mistakenly thought was purely decorative.

That got even Trix' attention. Her eyes didn't leave Sancho when Miguel yanked Mart's body out across her and beheaded him, too. But I watched as Miguel threw both heads at a third man, yelling, "Ponerlos en el hielo!"

Sancho's arms were around me, gently extracting me from the car. His fingers caressed my face, checking around my eyes. He kissed the small cut Mart's knife had left on my cheek. I remembered with a stab of yearning what it had felt like when our fingers had intermingled last time, and I had no longer known which fingers were whose.

"Don't know how it survived the tube, hitching a ride on the back of your mag car, but—"

"Sancho, no human can board that ship next week. I didn't mean to lie when I was here last time but—"

"Shhh." Those gentle fingers covered my mouth, then traced soft patterns on my lips. "We know. Now. As soon as we extract what data we can from those two heads, we'll know more."

"The aliens?"

"What they are is not their fault. We'll send even the sick ones home. But, thanks to your star drive, they will never return.

"After that we may work on resuming travel to Mars..."

He scooped me up in his arms then and started for the building. With all I'd been through I found all I could think of was how completely, overpoweringly wonderful it was to be held by a real, phys man. Now I could understand why Trix...

"Put me down!"

He looked hurt but complied.

"There's someone you must meet. Someone you must promise me you'll tell all about your sweet grandmother. Over and over again. Work on your words. Do it right. Do it until she can hear your grandmother's laugh."

He frowned.

I looked into myself, checking carefully after my last conversation with Reg. Yes, I could lie again. "I don't want you, Sancho. I'm a frigid bitch, spoiled by the porn sites. But here..." I turned around, dashed over to Trix, and pulled her over to him, "...is the dearest, sweetest creature in the world."

I got them talking, heading toward the building together. No, neither of them was going to fall in love that night, but I knew my beloved Trix. It was just a matter of time.

I walked back across the courtyard. That dog I'd seen before was coming in the opposite direction, followed by a whole roiling sea of fur. Suddenly I was attacked, pulled down and knocked over on my back yet again, smothered by unimaginably soft, sweet-smelling little bodies. Puppies. Merciless, they nuzzled my neck, licked my check, nipped playfully at my belly, and burrowed up under my clothes. Convulsed with giggles, I imagined my grin looked a lot like Teddy Roosevelt's. Phys... What a wonderful thing.

OTHER BOOKS BY
SUE HOLLISTER BARR

Boomers for the Stars
Craig Healing Springs
Ships
Twisted

ABOUT THE AUTHOR

Sue Hollister Barr's first publishing credits included articles in *The New York Times* and *Twisted*, a somewhat tongue-in-cheek horror novel first published conventionally in 1992 and still selling. "Holly" has also taught creative writing, with the blessings of state certification, and was senior editor for a literary agency for ten years. An avid fan of film, her favorites include *Piccadilly* (1929), *Trouble in Paradise* (1932), *His Girl Friday* (1940), *Sunset Boulevard* (1950), *Limelight* (1952), *To Kill a Mockingbird* (1962), *Blade Runner* (1982), *Brazil* (1985), *The Triplets of Belleville* (2003), and *Sita Sings the Blues* (2008). She maintains a weekly blog at suehollisterbarr.com.